CHUDEN KABIMO is based in Kalimpong. His short story collection, *1986,* centred on the Gorkhaland movement in that year, received the Sahitya Akademi Yuva Puraskar for Nepali language 2018. Originally written in Nepali, *Song of the Soil* is his first novel.

AJIT BARAL is based in Kathmandu. He is the author of *The Lazy Conman and Other Stories: Folktales from Nepal, Interviews Across Time and Space,* and co-author of *By the Way: Travels Through Nepal's Conflict* and *Shaili Pustak,* a Nepali style guide. Co-founder of FinePrint and the director of Nepal Literature Festival, he has also co-edited an anthology of Nepali short stories in English, *New Nepal, New Voices,* and is the editor of *First Love,* an anthology of memoirs.

CHUDEN KABIMO

SONG OF THE SOIL

A Novel

Translated from the Nepali by
Ajit Baral

BALESTIER PRESS
LONDON · SINGAPORE

Balestier Press
Centurion House, London TW18 4AX
www.balestier.com

Song of the Soil
Copyright © Chuden Kabimo, 2019
English translation copyright © Ajit Baral, 2021

First published in Nepali as *Faatsung* (फातसुङ) by FinePrint (Nepal) in 2019
This translation first published by FinePrint (Nepal) in 2021
This edition first published by Balestier Press in 2022

A CIP catalogue record for this book is available from the British Library.

ISBN 978 1 913891 21 3

This book is a work of fiction. The literary perceptions and
insights are based on experience, all names, characters, places,
and incidents either are products of the author's imagination
or are used fictitiously.

For Malbung,
where I took the first breath of my life.
Where I first cried, laughed, and dreamt.

EARTHQUAKE

"THEY'RE saying that Ripden is dead!"

The same sun whose fire singes the soles of your feet all day looks beautiful when it is about to set. For me, Ripden was that sole-burning sun that had set in the darkness created by the earthquake, throwing a part of my world into shadow.

*

It was a late Sunday afternoon.

The setting sun had reached a point beyond the Macfarlane Church. A cold wind was rushing past my ears. Kalimpong market was not crowded, perhaps because of the sudden chill. The girls who could be seen walking about in shorts and vests in the afternoon were returning home with their hands deep in their pockets. Taxi-drivers standing with their arms crossed near the Motor Stand were yawning.

I reached the crossroads at Damber Chowk from Ongden Road. The Industrial Park behind the Chowk was shut. Only a group of labourers was standing at the Chowk, busy splitting their wages for the day.

I did not feel like going home immediately and loitered there. The glow of happiness was shining on the labourers' faces. I basked in that glow for a moment.

Just then, a commotion erupted in the bazaar. The labourers ran off, screaming in different directions. The taxi-drivers fled too, yelling. It was then that I realised that the world was shaking.

I stood still for a long time.

The entire district of Darjeeling had just experienced a major earthquake.

The next day, I woke up late. I picked up the newspaper pushed underneath my door and read the headlines—the hills were in shambles.

The landslides had not abetted. Roads were broken in places. Tremors were still being felt and the telephone network was down.

It was eighteen hours after the earthquake that the mobile phone in my pocket buzzed. The call was from a new number. I answered it.

"Three dead bodies were found but none of them were of Ripden's. The landslide has swept away half the village," a voice cried softly over the phone. "You will have to come here and get the news of Ripden's death published in the newspaper. If not, the government won't accept that he is dead. You will come, won't you?"

The connection broke, and so did my heart. I went to the village.

Ripden had indeed died.

A heap of stones lay where Ripden's paradise-like house once stood. There was nothing but the sweeping landslide of terror in place of the patch of earth on which he first walked. In place of that stretch of sand on which he had etched his first letters, there was nothing but the sweeping mudslide of pain that was bearing everything away.

The mudslide that had followed the earthquake had swept away Ripden's house, sweeping away his dreams and his God.

How could Ripden be alive when everything else had been swept away? That was why the villagers had declared, "Ripden is certainly dead."

Two hours after making this declaration the villagers began to understand something else: "No corpse, no compensation."

Now, that was a big problem.

*

The sky was still overcast. The rain would stop for a moment and then continue to pour. Mudslides were tugging at the margins of the terraced fields, pulling them down. Fields were being torn apart and washed away; holes grew in them like winnowing sieves. The golden mustard fields began to resemble sodden biscuits. They looked just like Marie biscuits soaked in tea.

The mudslides had razed everything to the ground. The village was torn like a page out of an old book.

Pray, how was one to find Ripden's body in all of this?

The army did not manage to find Ripden's body even on the third day. In the eyes of the government Ripden had not died, even though he was dead in the eyes of the villagers.

The villagers had no option other than to follow the ancient practice. They searched for a piece of Ripden's old garment and set the final flame of the dagbatti[1] on it.

Everything had turned into ashes by the time I reached the village. I did not find even a whiff of smoke from the cloth that had been put to flame.

"Please get the news of Ripden's death written in a newspaper." The villagers laid out their final hopeful request before me. "The government isn't illiterate like us, right? Something or the other will be done, no?"

What was I to say?

Silently, I read their faces and remembered Ripden for one last time. I remembered his faded shorts, his nail-less toe, and his wrist lined with crusts of dirt. I remembered his hair that reached down to his ears, his plump cheeks, and the joyous days spent fifteen years ago.

---

[1] The ritual of setting the pyre on fire. Usually performed by the son or the nearest kin of the deceased.

Alphabets in Stone

THE river that flows throughout the year does so perennially and quietly. Only the bourn that dries up in winter shows off its power come monsoon season.

The Ghis river that swaggers in the monsoon was suffering in the throes of drought. Emerging reluctantly from a crevice in a hillside, it flowed down to the plains as though it was unwilling to do so.

Perched on the hill above this river was the village of Malbung, where morning began with the sun rising from Mangzing on the opposite hill. Twilight ended when the sun approached Barbot on the hill behind Malbung. The winds from Budhabare blew in winter and the rains from the plains poured in summer. The village would become inaccessible as soon as the monsoon month of Asār[2] began, and it would become parched with the arrival of Chaitra[3].

Opposite Malbung was the craggy village of Pokhrebung, which had been swept down low by a landslide. A bourn flowed right across this landslide, which would become mad like old man Budathoki's daughter during the monsoon, sweeping away anything that came in its way. Come winter, it would turn into a heap of stone and sand.

To the left of Pokhrebung stood Pubung, on whose shoulder

---

[2] Third month in the Nepali calendar.

[3] The last month in the Nepali calendar, beginning mid-March and ending in April.

flowed the Rankan in summer. Now only the remains of a landslide gleamed there.

I was watching the same mudslide with friends; we were sitting near Ripden's house. Ripden was doing something under the chicken coop. Suddenly, he stuck his head out and said, "Oi! Man is made of ash and chicken shit. If you think I'm lying, rub your hands and smell it."

I did as he asked. Others followed. My hands really did stink like chicken shit.

I rubbed them again. They stank even more.

But is man really made of ash and chicken shit? I did not believe it. Ripden understood that I did not believe him. Maybe that was why he added irritably, "It's true. It is written in the Bible."

He acted like he was trying to recollect something and said, "Do you want to hear the story?"

We all nodded. He began: "First, God created the sky. And then the earth. And then everything on earth. After creating everything, He thought, 'I need someone in my image to witness all this.' So on the sixth day, He made a human out of ash and chicken shit. That human was a boy. God put breath into that boy. Even after the boy was created, He felt that something was still missing on earth. It had everything, yet it lacked something. The flowers were blossoming, and yet the beauty of the earth felt incomplete. And then God made the boy fall into a deep slumber, took a rib out of his chest, and made a girl out of that rib. It was only then that the Earth became beautiful. And that is why men have one less rib than women. Understood?"

How could we not believe him, when he had told us about the very creation of the world?

I thought to myself, "Indeed, humans are made of ash and chicken shit. Ripden knows all! He really is our guru."

It was true. Ripden would always make new discoveries and tell us about them. He would tell us things we could never have thought of and make us gape at him in wonder.

He was the one who taught me to run off on my way to school. He was the one who made me an independent thinker. He was the one who taught me to live and not stay buried amongst textbooks.

I was enrolled in the Child Education Centre of the Rastriya Swayamsewak Sangh when I was seven years old. I was just learning to say, "Pranam Guruji" when Ripden taught me an important life lesson: "What is the use of reading and writing? If you can plough a field, you can eat a meal.'"

What better pretext for me to not study! Aama would walk with us for thirty minutes to reach the school and we would run away without staying there for even fifteen minutes.

A Miss and a Sir used to teach us. Sir was thin, so thin it seemed as though a strong wind would blow him away. His trousers hung loose from his frame. They would always be askew to the left, perhaps because he wore his belt too tight. An old pair of Galaxy slippers was the only footwear he could ever be seen wearing, and they too had worn thin.

Miss, on the other hand, was heavily built and would usually be clad in a kurta-suruwal. She would wear her hair loose and come to school with Fair and Lovely cream applied thickly on her face to conceal the pigmentation. We could smell the cream from afar.

Our school was more of a cowshed than school. It had doors on all sides. The bamboo slat fence that surrounded the school compound had fallen apart and was scattered all over, which is why we could slink away from whichever direction Ripden had signalled to us. On the first day, we ran away through the left door. On the second day, from the right. And on the third day, from the front. Sir did not even notice us!

On the fourth day, we had just reached the door when I saw Miss, with her powdered face, standing there. Her face had become red and her eyes were bulging.

"Oi truants!" Miss shouted, beside herself with rage. She

complained to my mother who had walked me to school as usual, "Ripden has spoilt your son, he's always running away. Yesterday, they skipped school to steal cucumbers. They ate them even before the first harvest had been offered at the church. We have received a complaint!"

Mother spanked me twice with a bamboo slat. My voice quivered and I pissed my pants. My eyes became moist and pitiable.

I remembered Ripden chanting, "Bitter bitter go go, sweet sweet come come," as he cut the pilfered cucumber. Miss announced a new punishment: "You both will do fifty squats."

Lo, had the "sweet sweet" not come?

Ripden turned red. For a second, it seemed like he would not oblige. But there was no alternative.

I held on to his ears and he to mine as we began our squats. By the tenth repetition, I began to pant. My legs trembled. We had just reached the count of twenty when my legs gave up and I fell down. Tears blinded my eyes.

"That's enough," I heard Miss say just as I began to see stars. "Never run away from school! Never steal cucumbers! Or else you will have to crawl on your knees."

Ripden stared blankly for a moment. Then he came up to me and whispered, smirking, "I'll have to run away from school only if I come here, won't I? You too shouldn't come. Did the elephant become so big because it studied in school?"

On our way back from school, he made me swear on knowledge itself: "From tomorrow, we may lose our lives, but we will not attend school."

It was the day after we made that promise that Ripden started to take the goats out to graze. He would go to the jungle carrying my grandfather's bag.

For three days, I was taken to school by force. But no, I did not feel like staying, so I would run away as soon as I could.

How could I study when my guru Ripden wasn't with me?

On the fourth day, my grandfather Baje finally declared, "Let him attend school later. He is still too small. And he doesn't have his friend there."

Only then was I relieved!

It must have been a few months later that Ripden delivered a religious sermon, "Rub your forehead one hundred and eight times. The image of Lord Buddha will be formed on it."

I didn't know how to count. If Ripden knew how, he might have counted for me, like Miss did when we were doing the squats. But he didn't, which meant that I could not rub my forehead for exactly one hundred and eight times. That was why the image of Lord Buddha didn't appear on my forehead. Rather, a bruise did.

*

My friends—Sonam Tamang, Ongden Lepcha, Taarnam Bhujel, Gairi Bhai, Tularam Sharma, Juniram Chhetri, Hari Prasad Bishwokarma—were still busy rubbing their hands. Sniffing their hands, they said, "Yes indeed. It smells exactly like chicken shit."

I gloated. Guru Ripden was standing nearby and laughing.

"Oi, have a bath," said Baje, who was sitting in the courtyard weaving a doko basket out of strips of bamboo bark. He issued a decree. "We have to attend a wedding tomorrow."

It was the winter month of Baisakh[4]. The only food that was being cooked at home was either millet porridge or tasteless bulgur. We had not seen white rice for a long time. It was then that the chance of eating at a wedding reception had presented itself. All our faces brightened.

Hari Prasad came up with an idea. "Let's go down to the Ghis river. We will wash ourselves thoroughly. If you rub with a dalsing stone, the dirt will come off easily. That stone is white, that's why."

---

[4] The first month in the Nepali calendar.

"Go, go," Baje said, smiling.

We left for the river. When we were about to reach Kimbugairi, Ripden said, "Boys, we should eat three times tomorrow. Mula! The marriage is in a Chhetri household. They serve only two pieces of meat each. If we eat thrice, we will get six pieces each."

"Why do you say that?" Juniram asked, getting upset.

But the rest of us agreed loudly with Ripden. "Yes, we will eat thrice!"

The next day, the sound of the panché baja, the five auspicious musical instruments, resonated in the air.

We watched the marriage procession while standing on the edge of a field terrace. It climbed up the hill from Pairetaar.

Two old men were walking in front, carrying something that looked like the branches of a cherry tree. Following them were people carrying thekis carved out of wood. Behind them walked the shehnai players. Uff! How could they dance on such a narrow trail! And these people were dancing shamelessly even in a village full of strangers. Some were singing too. Juniram informed us, "They're not singing songs but reciting shlokas[5]."

A few young women were walking behind the rest. In their midst was a tall boy—the groom. He had a red tika on his forehead and a bright smile on his lips. The radiance of happiness gleamed in his eyes and a striking turban was perched on his head. Another thin boy tagged along with the groom, carrying an umbrella. The boy would hurry after him wherever he went. It was as if the groom was his king for the day. The shade of the umbrella must always reach the groom. The heat of the sun should not singe the king even a little!

We walked behind the procession. Ripden, who was up in front, would occasionally turn back and wink at us. Juniram found a reason to gloat and whispered in my ear, "Now you see how grand a

---

[5] A verse of lines in Sanskrit, typically recited as a prayer.

Chhetri marriage is! A Lepcha marriage is nothing compared to it, nothing! They're saying that the bride is beautiful too. My mother said that no one in the village is as beautiful as her. Didn't you see the postcard of the Samjhana film the other day? They're saying she is as beautiful as Tripti Nadakar, the heroine of that film!"

"Mula, is it enough to just have music?" Ripden exclaimed. "Think of the food and drink they treat you to at Lepcha weddings. Only at Lepcha weddings can the Chhetris and the Bahuns get very drunk!"

Juniram ran off in a huff. Ripden followed.

The boy who was carrying an umbrella over the groom's head was having a hard time. The path was narrow. The way wound uphill at times. And to top it off, the groom was tall.

The people in the procession were sweating profusely.

They finally reached the bride's home after an hour and a half. After that, we didn't care where the marriage party went. We busied ourselves drinking tea and eating selroti.

It was some time after we had reached the bride's home that our family members arrived.

"You all better behave!" Baje decreed.

Ripden gestured to us. We made our escape.

Straw had been spread out on the terraced field immediately below the marriage house. Small shops had been set up where paan and savouries such as dalmut, fried gram and peas were available. How I used to enjoy eating dalmut! But I didn't have any money to buy it. Ripden came up with an idea: "Drunkards sometimes drop their money here and there. We just have to walk around looking for it."

Our eyes began to scan the ground.

We searched for money for half an hour, but we did not manage to find even a paisa!

Music was booming at full volume from the marriage house. Cooks were busy preparing food at one end of the millet field. At its upper corner, the women stitching plates out of leaves were teasing each other.

A bunch of boys were standing on one edge of the field. Ripden said, signalling to us, "Let's go there. It looks like they are distributing food."

It must have been nearly one o'clock. The sun was right on top of our heads. We ran towards where Ripden had indicated. When we reached, we found that they had started serving the food to the children early. They said they were doing so to thin out the crowd. We forgot the money. We forgot the fried gram, the peas and the dalmut.

"Aren't you boys from the Lepcha village? Your food has been prepared down there. Go!" Mantare Kaka sounded an order. He had recognised us. We were relieved. We jumped down to the lower field, took our leaf plates and stood in a queue.

How could we be content with just a single helping? Half an hour later, we were standing on the straw, holding another leaf plate.

An hour elapsed just like that. The sun had cast its shadow on the hill opposite. It looked as though the weather was about to turn cool.

"How about eating with the elders next?" Ripden suggested this to us when the music suddenly stopped to invite the elders to eat.

The announcer said without preamble, "Our Lepcha brothers, please proceed to the lower field. The Shehnai party, please head there too. The Chhetri group, please come to the upper field."

Did we need anything after that insult? Baje, trembling with rage, asked, "Why should we go to the lower field? You did the same thing to us last time, calling us beef eaters. We will boycott the weddings of Chhetris and Bahuns from now on. Let's go back."

Baje was the president of the Kyong Sejum, the Lepcha association. Everyone agreed with him. The Lepchas decided to leave without eating.

Attempts were made to settle the matter, but nothing worked.

The Lepchas were adamant.

Baje thundered, "Oi sahamsong! Aba di. Li nong gatsi." (Oi, you gluttons! Come here. We are going back.)

We followed Baje without making a fuss. Baje made another declaration, "They insult us because we are illiterate. They think of us as beef-eating illiterates. You shall all go to school from tomorrow. You must all study!"

I nodded. Ripden turned around and brought his mouth near my ear, "See, you got to eat twice because of me. Otherwise, we would all have returned hungry!"

I turned red just thinking about it.

I looked around. Juniram was following me.

"Only the Lepchas are going back home," I asked him, scratching my head. "Why did you come, Juniram?"

"Friendship above caste," Juniram declared, smiling broadly. He ran off, baring his unbrushed yellow teeth.

*

It was a week after the declaration of the boycott that we were taken to school again.

The school was in Biga. I had to walk for an hour and a half to get there. The school building was made of wood but there wasn't any hole to slink through.

There was a new teacher. His hair was curly, like that of the Italian footballer Roberto Baggio. His eyes were not like those of the Miss from the previous school. His body was not as thin as that of the Sir in the previous school. But his voice was soft. He looked at me and smiled. Then he drew a figure with a long tail on the bench and said, "Go get pebbles for me and put them over this figure."

I went out. Ripden was already picking up stones. Seeing me, he said, "Let's run away."

"What did you say?" A loud voice boomed out from behind us. I turned. Sir was standing there looking at me. I almost lost my senses. Ripden ran back into the class.

I feigned innocence and picked up a handful of pebbles. I went inside and put them over the outline of the figure. When all the pebbles in my hand had run out, the figure was complete. Pointing at it, Sir said, "This is the first letter of the alphabet: 'ka', understood?"

It was only some days later that I realised I had been enrolled in primary school at the start of the monsoon season. That explained the "pebble" class.

I then went up to "A" and dropped down to "B". Yet I managed to get to Class 1 in the first year, though the promotion was due to my height rather than my intelligence.

The Dreams of the Village

THE most important thing in life is to recognise the alphabet "ka", to understand "ka". Thereafter you understand everything else yourself.

I realised this when I reached Class 4.

It was around that time that Miss came to the village.

It was on a Sunday. The sun had emerged after a period of rain. The villagers were busy planting rice. Miss reached the school exhausted.

Miss was tall. She was wearing big earrings. I watched them swing as she walked. Whenever she spoke, a smile would break out on her face before the words came. She was carrying a black bag that contained a thick book inside. A word was written in big bold letters on the cover—"Bible".

I really liked the cover of the book.

Miss walked straight up to me. She gently pinched my cheek and asked, "Do you like the Bible?"

Her hair was silky, like that of Prince Siddhartha, or Lord Buddha in his childhood, judging from the picture in our textbook.

"A new Miss has come." The news spread throughout the village. The villagers were busy planting rice, but they stopped work and rushed to the school to welcome her.

Miss was delighted to see the villagers. She forgot that she was tired. Forcing a laugh she exclaimed, "Uff, this place is so remote, it is like Kalapani[6]!"

The villagers were amazed to see Miss too, as no one ever comes to the village except during elections. Those who somehow arrive leave quickly, vowing to never come back again. Because the village does not have paved roads. Or electricity. Or a hospital.

Miss was, in fact, the first person who had arrived before an election. That is why her words drew the whole village to her. All the villagers declared in one voice, "Miss likes our place. She compared it to Kalapani!"

"We now have a sir and a miss at the school," Baje said, smiling. "Our children won't have to remain illiterate anymore."

A week after her arrival, she told us her life-story: "I was born in Kalimpong. I grew up and studied in Darjeeling. It seems a person becomes a part of whichever place she is most familiar with. That's why I became like someone who has always lived in Darjeeling. Nowadays, I find even the bazaar in Kalimpong empty and unappealing. After finishing higher secondary school, I went back to Kalimpong and got a job. The appointment letter said that my posting was in Dalapchand Primary School. I was relieved because the school was near town. I happily went to the school to take up the job. But once I got there, I learnt that it was not my school; my school was the Second Dalapchand Primary School. Dalapchand in Biga!"

We all fell silent. She smiled a little. Pushing back her hair, she started to speak again, "It was then that I understood: my school is in a village where there are no roads, no electricity, no hospital, not even a shop. I was so dispirited that I decided to resign.

"At that time, my grandfather, who is a retired teacher, arrived. He took my hands in his and said, 'There is nothing there, but it has immense possibilities. It is a Lepcha village. You shall teach their

---

[6] A colonial prison located in the Andaman Islands where the British incarcerated freedom fighters during the Independence Movement.

new generation. This is a test for you. God himself is testing you. If you don't go to that village, no one will. Child, you shall go there. You shall teach that village to read, to speak, to dream. I will be happy the day the village starts to dream. My dear granddaughter, do you understand what I am saying?'

"Baje stopped. I started breaking down. I changed my mind and came here. When I arrived here, I realised that our Raju-sir is just a volunteer and is returning home for good!

"But even if I am alone, I will make you capable enough to dream." Miss took a deep breath.

Listening to Miss, I understood: Our village hasn't seen many things. Most importantly, it hasn't dreamt any dreams.

What more did we need? The dream that Miss had talked about began to haunt us. She would make us think more than she would make us read.

*

"Get on the stage and talk about yourself," Miss ordered us.

I shuddered. My voice sank. At other times, I would shout at the top of my voice. But up on stage, not a single word came out of my mouth. Instead, tears dripped from my eyes. Everyone started to laugh.

It turned out Ripden had pissed his shorts. He could not even utter a squeak. Hari Prasad could only manage to say his name. Juniram said "namaskar" loudly enough for everyone to hear but what he said thereafter, even he did not know.

Whatever it was, we were relieved. Because all of us had failed!

Silence pervaded the classroom. In that silence, Miss walked up to the stage and said, beaming, "You should try a hundred times, the miracle will happen at least once. Because we are on the same earth where a caterpillar turns into a butterfly overnight."

We didn't understand what she had said, yet we clapped noisily.

*

Two weeks later Miss said, giving us each a sheet of plain paper, "Draw the kind of village you want yours to be ten years from now and show it to me. Learn to imagine. Please sit and draw."

We took the papers. This wasn't as difficult as speaking on stage. Our hearts didn't race and our legs didn't tremble. But still, there was another problem. We had to imagine before we began drawing. But wasn't it a huge thing for us, who couldn't even dream, to let our imaginations soar? And yet, we started.

Miss came into the room after half an hour. She took up my drawing book first. I began to tremble again.

Miss looked at my faint, unclear sketch. There was a footpath drawn in pencil. There were copses of trees on both sides of the footpath. The school was there too. On top of the building was a hall.

"Good."

I leapt in excitement, for I had received an unexpected word of appreciation.

It was Ripden's turn next. A big sun shone in his drawing. There were more houses in the village than we now had. Flowers were blooming too, but they were bigger than the houses. Still, a road had reached his village.

Miss smiled a little and repeated the earlier word: "Good."

It was then I understood: Miss would assign "good" to everyone's efforts. I had jumped for joy for nothing!

Juniram's imaginary village was crowded with houses. All the people were busy. It looked like they were all headed to the Public Distribution Centre to collect their rations. A temple had come up on the edge of the village. "Jai Shriram" was written on its door.

Miss smiled again and walked up to Hari Prasad. She looked at his drawing book and then kept staring at his drawing for a long time. She was flabbergasted. She exclaimed that his drawing was like that of an artist's!

What is a artist? Who knew?

We all crowded around and looked at his drawing of the village.

The village was beautiful. White clouds were scudding over it. Underneath the clouds the Ghis river flowed, aiming its course at the plains of the Madhesh.

A little above the village was our school. There was another structure above the school. The words "High School" were written on that building. A house had been etched a little further away. That was the health centre.

This was a terrific vision! That day, he had dreamt up something that the villagers have been incapable of dreaming of for a decade.

Miss patted his back and said to all of us, "You are the engineers who will build this village. You must fulfil the dreams of your village."

*

15th August was approaching.

Miss made another declaration, "We will organise a big programme."

We were thrilled.

Miss said, "Gyan Tshering and Ramesh have left the school. Now only four of you are in Class 4 and next year you will join high school. So, all four of you have to participate in the programme. It is compulsory. All of you will have to give a speech from the stage. Whoever gives a good speech will get additional marks. This programme is a part of your work education and physical education classes, and you don't have to submit handwork this time. Do you understand?"

I trembled again. Ripden's face turned red. That was how his face was: it always turned red whenever he was frightened or angry.

Only Hari Prasad looked happy. Maybe that was why he smiled. Juniram's face too had darkened.

"What are the good things about your village, what are its shortcomings, and who do you want to be in the future," Miss continued. "You will have to speak on these three topics.

Understood?"

As soon as Miss uttered those words, all of us started to walk our own separate paths, thinking our own separate thoughts.

While one of us would secretly go to the stage to practice his speech, the other would be seen deeply engrossed in thought. Another one would have questions to ask the rest of us about one thing or another.

It was as if we were like the digits of the same hand. The only difference was the size of each finger, and we were about to demonstrate that to the whole village.

*

The stage was ready. The programme was about to begin.

Raju-sir was on one side of the stage. This time he hadn't dyed his hair black. One could distinctly spot the grey strands. In the middle sat our Chief Guest, the Mandal—the head of the village—looking radiant. He often attended programmes a little drunk.

Miss was on the other side. The villagers were scattered all over the ground in front of the stage. They looked as serious as they would when they were listening to speeches during the elections.

The Master of Ceremonies went up the stage, welcomed everyone, and gave a background of the programme. He then called out the first name on the list. That name was mine.

I climbed the stage with a piece of paper in hand and started to read:

"Baje loves me most of all. But what can I say, he drinks too much. Earlier, Sainla Baje, his brother, used to live with us. Sainla Baje couldn't laugh or weep without alcohol. There was a chakra on his palm. When he was a small boy, a lama had examined his hand and said, 'He will either become a king or a beggar.'

"That was what happened. Sainla Baje always drank too much. And he had to have meat with his drink. He would try to beat up those who advised him against drinking.

"One day, a bullock belonging to Funyel-ba fell off a cliff. The news spread all over the village. Sainla Baje ran towards the commotion.

"'Take the meat. But give me half of the price later, okay? It was a big bullock but what to do now?' Funyel-ba said softly. 'What curse has befallen us! Sainla, I am leaving this to your care.'

"Sainla Baje was happy. He distributed the meat to everyone in the village. He set aside one full doko of meat for the family. We ate it for a whole week. He would get drunk and go around punching people. It was at that time that he broke his left hand in a contest, trying to chip the bark off a needlewood tree with his fist.

"A month thus passed. And then a new problem came up. Everyone had eaten the meat, but no one had paid for it.

"Sainla Baje began to go mad with worry. Just then, Funyel-ba arrived. Baje hurriedly showed him two doko full of ginger.

"Everyone said that Funyel-ba was a greedy man. But he was not. He said, 'Sow the ginger. We will share the crop later once it grows.'

"Baje sowed the ginger and produced double the expected harvest. He shared the produce with Funyel-ba. While the ginger was being shared, Funyel-ba said, hacking phlegm out of his throat, 'Sainla, don't use the seed-ginger. Sow it yourself. We can share it next year. It yields well under your care.'

"With those two doko of ginger he produced more and shared it with Funyel-ba. But he still couldn't cover the price of the meat—he was told that interest had been added to the price.

"That year when the interest was added, all the ginger rotted. Sainla Baje started to drink more and began to lose his mind. Just then, Funyel-ba made an appearance and said, 'You are from our very own village. Don't worry. Give me that hilltop field. I will waive off everything and give you an extra fifty rupees.'

"Now Sainla Baje became king. He drank for one whole month. After that, he started to carve out his land and sell it, one plot at a time. He would get drunk day in, day out with the money he received. All his money would be spent within a month. And then he would become pitiful.

"He would become a king when he sold his land and a beggar when he ran out of that money.

"Sainla Baje died because of drinking. This is why I don't like the villagers getting drunk. Nor do I like them selling their land to get drunk."

There was loud applause. I was floating with happiness. I started again:

"Politics always betrays the dreams of a village. I want to write the story of those dreams. I want to study and become a writer."

The whole ground echoed with louder applause and cheer.

It was Ripden's turn next. He began in a confident tone:

"I don't like my villagers cutting grass. And cleaning cow dung. I would really like to see a road come to our village. I will study to become a soldier. I will serve the country. That's all."

And then came Juniram. He said:

"In our village, there isn't even a road for people to walk on. There is no electricity either. In fact, it doesn't have anything. I don't like this village. It lacks everything. In every election, leaders come to us and say that they will build a bridge over the Ghis river. But no one has done anything. That's why people die, they're swept away by the river trying to cross it in the monsoon. I don't like all of this at all. Still, no one in this village tries to bring the other down. That, I like. I will study to become a leader. I will build a bridge over the Ghis river."

The villagers liked what the "leader" had said. Everyone clapped loudly. And then Hari Prasad Bishwokarma was called up. Miss smiled. She must have done so because she was confident that he who could draw so wonderfully would think deeply too.

Hari Prasad walked to the stage and poured his heart out:

"I am a low-caste boy, aren't I? I don't like others saying this to me. Just the day before yesterday, Purohit-ba scolded me, saying I must not go near his granddaughter. Am I not allowed to go near my friend? She is younger than me. Still, they say I have to address her as 'timi' while she should address me as 'tan'. When I hear these things, I feel like crying. In the last Naagpanchami festival, Purohit-ba went to everyone's house and pasted the naag with the picture of serpents on their doors. But he called me out to the road, gave me the naag and yelled at me, saying that I should paste the naag on our door myself.

"Tell me, am I not afraid of snakes?

"The year before last, my father had been asked to make an idol of Shiva-ji. My father made it, working day and night. The idol looked exactly like Shiva-ji. Purohit-ba was standing nearby, watching. Ba started to make the serpent around the neck of the god without taking off his slippers.

"You know, I am very afraid of snakes. That is why I had run off to the edge of the courtyard and sat there. Just then, Purohit-ba screamed all of a sudden, 'Bastard, how dare you go near God wearing slippers?'

"I love my father very much. I cannot watch anyone shout at him!

"My younger uncle plays the shehnai. If he stops playing, no wedding will take place in the village. My maternal uncle sews clothes. If he stops, Dashain[7] won't arrive in the village. My elder uncle makes implements day and night. If he stops, all work in the village will stop. I think that without my younger uncle or my maternal uncle, my elder uncle or my ba, this village won't function. The world itself won't function. That, I like.

"And Raju-sir says it is only the Hindus who have upper and lower castes. Among the Christians, everyone is equal. I will become a Christian after finishing my studies."

Everyone laughed. Hari Prasad climbed down from the stage, turning blue with embarrassment.

---

[7] Major festival in the Hindu religion.

It was on that day when Hari Prasad said that he would become a Christian that Raju-sir turned to one side and smiled. I still have not forgotten that. In fact, that was the last time he smiled. After that, he taught us for three or four months unsmilingly and disappeared from the village.

Three months after he disappeared, a shakha—branch—of the Rastriya Swayamsevak Sangh, the National Volunteers' Organisation, was set up on the school playground.

Neelkamal was the pramukh—chief—of the shakha. For some time, he taught us how to wield fighting sticks. He made us do two Surya Namaskars. He raised the slogan: "Bharat Mata ki Jai!"

We too shouted along with him: "Bharat Mata ki Jai!"

The session at the shakha finally ended.

And then?

Neelkamal came up to us and made a shocking revelation, "It was Raju-sir who killed Ripden's appa. Did you know?"

Fever

WHY did Raju-sir kill Ripden's appa?

My senses deserted me when I heard what Neelkamal had said. My legs went limp. My mouth grew parched. I ran to the waterspout and held my head under the water. I gulped down some water. I realised that I had left my fighting stick back at the shakha.

"How is Ripden feeling?" I thought. I wanted to see him.

He had quietly left for home without telling anyone. I felt very bad for him. The friends who stand with you in times of joy can hardly be called friends; it is the friends who stay with you in times of sorrow who are real friends.

I have never experienced pain without having Ripden by my side. Pain came regularly to me. At times in the form of a bamboo cane, at other times in the form of squats. Or in having to kneel in punishment. In whatever form pain visited, Ripden was always with me. Now that he was himself in great pain, how could I leave him alone?

I had heard that someone who has disappeared never dies. There is always someone who waits, strewing the grains of hope on the ground, and in whose eyes the disappeared appears every evening, just before the sun sets.

Ripden's appa had disappeared. That was why he would sit waiting, having strewn the grains of hope on the ground. And his father would come—as a memory.

Would Ripden's appa never return?

"Ripden, don't cry. I am with you," I repeated these words to myself as I ran off to meet him.

His house was quiet. His aku—uncle—was in the cowshed below. Evening had already fallen. The kids hadn't been herded into the goat shed. Even the chicken coop was still open.

I went straight to his room. It was dark inside. Someone was lying down, wrapped up in a blanket. I lit a lamp. It was Ripden.

I looked at him closely. His eyes were red and his face pale. His legs were bent and had been drawn together under the blanket.

"What happened to you?" I asked him.

"I am about to die of fever," he quavered. He turned to his left and coughed, shaking.

I touched his forehead. Baaf re! How hot it was!

"He has no one to look after him at this time." My mind whirled.

His mother had left him when he was four years old. His appa too had disappeared in the revolution. No, he hadn't disappeared; he had died, which was now confirmed. Ripden lived with his aku but aku lived with his booze.

If Ripden had anything with him, it was hope. And it was on that road of hope that his appa walked. Now that road too no longer existed.

I had a few myrobalan seeds in my pockets. I gave him one and said, "Here, eat this. It will cure your cough."

He sat there with the seed in his hand.

I said, "Appa died a long time ago. Why do you worry about him now? If you stop worrying, your fever will go away. Do you understand?"

He didn't listen to me and turned to the other side again.

He coughed for some time, then turned his head towards me and looked me directly in the eye.

"Are you missing your appa?" I asked softly.

"You cunt! Don't make me laugh!" Biting a corner of the blanket, he asked, "Will you go to Lolay with me tomorrow?"

I was about to tell him that someone so sick shouldn't walk when

Neelkamal's words slipped into my mind: "His father's sister lives there. Some of his appa's friends are also there."

I replied slowly, "You will get well tomorrow only if you stop worrying. And if you get well, I will go with you. Let's not go to school, okay?"

"Will you really go with me?" he poked his head out of the blanket and asked.

"You get well first," I said, touching his head. "God's promise, I will go with you tomorrow. I will bunk off the exams too."

"Then you go home now," he said, his voice getting firmer. "I will get well and come to your house tomorrow."

Baaf re! What confidence!

I kept staring at him. Then I quietly walked home.

*

"Baje, I will go to Lolay with Ripden," I said, screwing up my courage early in the morning.

"You will not go to Lolay!" Baje was churning buttermilk. He skimmed the butter off the surface with his hand and turned to me.

"I will sneak off if you don't let me. Poor Ripden is about to die," I thought to myself.

"They say Raju-sir killed Ripden's appa in the revolution. Is that true?" I asked. My tears nearly fell, but I blinked them back just in time.

"Donkey! Don't talk nonsense so early in the morning." Baje sat down gingerly on a low stool. "Yesterday's hatchlings, what do you know about the revolution?"

"But everyone says so!"

"His father wasn't murdered. He disappeared on his own." Baje's face darkened. "A disappeared person never dies. That is why his appa isn't yet dead, get it?"

"Raju-sir killed him. That was what Neelkamal said." I was

becoming weepy.

"You won't understand these things. Neelkamal has his own agenda. He doesn't want Sir to come back again, that's why he said that. Your Miss too will soon be posted to another place. Women cannot stay in a remote place like this for long. Neelkamal is playing games to get Miss to leave early and ensure that Sir never returns. He wants to be the teacher. If a Class 9-failed man becomes a teacher, what will happen to the school, tell me? No one killed Ripden's appa!"

"So what should I do then?" The love I felt for Ripden still tugged at me. "I cannot see Ripden cry. They say that Ripden's appa's friends are in Lolay."

Baje paused for a moment and then stroked my face.

From time to time, Baje would narrate to us the pain of leaving the village. He had left home only for three days in his life. And those were the only days he had suffered. Those were the only three days that he had to go without food. That was why he would always say, "You will suffer if you leave home."

Whenever talk of the town would crop up, he would start recounting the same story of suffering. In the story, he would leave the village to stick posters. There was a faded document from that time, which was created by the State Reorganization Commission. On that document the word "Lepcha" had been written on a map of Darjeeling from 1956. Baje would show that and speak about the struggles of demanding a separate state in 1970.

Baje didn't say anything this time. Lolay isn't a town either, but a village. Maybe that was why he didn't repeat his story.

"I will go, okay?" I said for the last time.

"If you attend school, you will understand things. You shouldn't go to the town; you will only find grief there," Baje said, coughing. "Don't insist on going. Ripden's appa disappeared in the revolution of '86. In fact, he had gone to study with Raju-sir but the revolution happened right at that time. He got involved in it and disappeared.

What's the point of searching for him now?"

Baje lit a bangali and turning away, exhaled a plume of smoke.

I was in a state of confusion.

I did not know what to do. Just then, Ripden arrived. That same boy who was bedridden with fever until yesterday had become a new person. He had applied vegetable oil to his hair and parted it in the middle. The oil stank.

"I am running off." He first winked at me and then called me to the back of the house. "Quick, let's hurry. I know the way."

Baje was still churning buttermilk with his back to me. Aama had gone off to collect fodder. My love for Ripden made the decision. I picked up an old second-hand sweater, wore a pair of worn-out slippers, and ran off after him. I reached the waterspout at the speed of the wind. There I washed my face. I tried to clean my legs, but the dirt wouldn't come off. I put on a pair of trousers over my half-pants and set off.

*

We had climbed up to quite a height before I took a good look at his face. It was shrivelled up yesterday, but today it was glowing. The feeling that I was the one who had made my friend well again made me strangely happy. I asked, "Ripden, how much do you love your father?"

He walked steadily and silently up the hill. We had to walk the whole day. It wasn't easy to reach Relli, was it?

We were about to reach the village of Pemling.

"Oi, slow down. You were burning with fever yesterday," I said. "You might have a relapse."

He stopped for a moment, picked up a stone and threw it, aiming at a tree. He then ran uphill and said, "I hadn't prepared for the exam at all. That's why I slept with an onion in my armpit so I would come down with fever. But in the evening our plans changed so I threw the onion away. Now all this fever-shever won't relapse. Got it?"

"Motherfucker!" I exclaimed. How angry I was!

*

We walked silently through the day.

It was sunset by the time we crossed the jungle. My stomach had started to churn out of hunger. Thoughts of my grandfather began to haunt me. Memories of my mother began to dance before my eyes.

There was a waterspout beside the road. We drank until our thirst was quenched. We wiped our tears, which were about to fall. We walked for two more hours and reached Matim's home late in the evening.

Matim, Ripden's father's elder sister-in-law, was nearly spooked when she saw us.

"Did you run away from home?" she challenged without even offering us tea.

"No, we were sent here from home." Who could keep up with Ripden?

It was seven in the evening. The radio station Akashvani started to wheeze out the news with difficulty. A voice would become audible and then it would vanish. Ripden sat dozing near the fireplace.

The news bulletin ended. Matim entered the kitchen. Behind her was a middle-aged man. On his face was a bushy beard and he wore old slippers on his feet. He was wearing shorts even in the cold. I looked at his wrinkled forehead; it reminded me of the fallows near our house. I looked at the calluses all over his hands; they reminded me of the days when I used to walk barefoot.

Matim gestured. Ripden joined his palms to greet namaste. I did the same.

"He is my nephew," Matim said, pouring black tea into glasses. "Norden's son, don't you remember?"

"Norden?" His mouth remained agape for a long time. "His son is all grown up!"

Norden?

My ears rang. My face reddened and my ears became hot. I said slowly, "Do you know his appa?"

The bearded man would speak softly. He would often think of something and scrunch up his face, but it would brighten up through sheer force of will. The colour of the sky and the human mind are alike. You never know when they will change.

"He is your uncle," Matim said, gesturing at the bearded man. "And moreover, he is also a friend of Ripden's appa. He injured his leg during the revolution. He now spends his days breaking rocks at the Relli river. He sleeps here at night."

The reference to the revolution caught my attention. I went up to sit near the bearded man.

Matim gave the bearded man a glass of locally brewed raksi[8]. He opened up a little after he finished drinking. He came near Ripden and caressed his cheek.

We were very hungry. Matim gave us some fried rice.

"They say Raju-sir killed his appa. Is that so?" I whispered into the bearded man's ear, "Tell us the truth. Did his appa disappear or was he murdered?"

The bearded man's face crumpled up all at once. His eyes shut. His hand reached up to his forehead. Then he smiled a little. He took yet another glass of raksi and swigged it in one gulp.

And then?

---

[8] Local homemade alcohol.

WE WILL GIVE UP OUR LIVES

ALLAHU Akbar . . . !
The clouds impeded the voice that drifted towards the sky. The voice was then buffeted by the wind which brought it to the roof of Nasim's house. It dropped down from the roof and right into his room. Just as the voice dropped inside, Nasim's abba called out, "Oi Nasim! Come for namaaz."

It was evening. Nasim entered the room lazily. He spread a white sheet on the floor and kneeled on it. He held his hands in front of himself, faced west and began reciting the namaaz prayer.

His father had instructed that reciting the namaaz was to become accomplished. He had said, "You can do whatever you like the rest of the time, but recite the namaaz at least five times a day. Because that is Allah's order. The same Allah who created earth and eighteen thousand beings. He created humans too, the being closest to his heart. Which is why an ideal person must recite the namaaz five times a day."

Once Abba finished, he turned to Nasim.

Nasim was still busy invoking Allah. For the first time, Abba thought to himself, "The boy will now get back on track." He then coughed twice and said, "To give pain to someone is to sin. You do understand, don't you? In the eyes of Allah, to give pain to oneself is also to sin. Don't do anything wrong ever, even unwittingly. Allah is everywhere, he sees everything. The best and the purest names in the world are the names of Allah. Have you understood?"

A thought raced through Nasim's mind: "Does Allah also

know that we beat up the school captain in the afternoon?" He remembered his best friend Norden. Norden had come from the village to be admitted into Class 5; he lived with Raju-sir.

Norden used to say he was from Paari, the hills across the valley on the far side of the Relli river. Which place was this Paari? How was Nasim to know? All he understood was this: Norden was weak in mathematics. He used to live with Sir and study with him.

Norden used to wear his scarf in the style of Dev Anand, the actor. He would brag to whoever he met that he was the Mandal's son. And if riled, he could beat up students from Class 9.

"Norden. What a lovely name," Nasim thought. "This too must be one of Allah's names. But why does he go around beating people?"

The day's incident came alive in his mind.

"No, he fights because he wants to help others."

*

It was before tiffin break. Nasim had started to make mischief in class. He tore out pages from his exercise book, crumpled them into balls, and threw them at Sitaram's back. Those sitting behind him laughed riotously.

The school captain had come to the classroom and ordered everyone to not make noise. The captain's name was Garjaman Gurung. Everyone used to call him Garjé. With a name like Garjé, which meant the Roarer, everyone was afraid of him.

Garjé was beside himself with anger.

He went up to Nasim and slapped him twice. Nasim's head nearly hit a bench. Another slap landed on Nasim's face. Tears flowed from his eyes. He turned to the left. Clenching his fist, he swore on his mother's life to take revenge on Garjé. As soon as school got over, he ran off to seek Norden's help.

The only thing Norden wanted to ever do was to show off his

strength. And this was the perfect opportunity. "Give me your tiffin. I will need more strength to beat him up. That mule has a big body." The last thing Nasim wanted to do after being slapped was to eat, and so he gave his tiffin to Norden. After eating, Norden flexed his right arm like a bodybuilder, flaunting his bicep, and said, "I will beat him Bruce Lee-style. You just wait and see."

As soon as the final bell struck, Norden readied himself to pounce on the captain.

There was a meadow in front of the school and the school playground was right below it. To the left of the playground was a barren field, where weeds were sprouting. A dense bamboo grove grew to one side of the field. Norden leapt towards the bamboo grove, shouting. As soon as he saw Norden bounding towards him, the school captain's swagger disappeared. His legs went limp. His eyes turned dewy.

"It won't be good for you if you touch the school captain," Garjé managed feebly. When he heard Garjé's voice shudder, Norden's courage knew no bounds.

Whenever he would be filled with arrogance, Norden used to remember what his batim, his father's elder brother, had said to him when he was small: "Remember, we belong to a family of Mandals." Today, Norden became the son of a Mandal. "My mother is a Bhotini, do you understand? My uncle is a butcher. And I eat beef. Do you want to fight me now?"

Norden advanced towards Garjé, grabbed his shirt lapel and shouted, "You swine! You dare beat up the weak? Come fight me if you can."

His voice drifted up towards the sky. Fists swung in the air. The captain did not manage to even blink an eye. Two blows landed on his face.

"I will tell Sir tomorrow," the captain said, standing up slowly. Norden leapt and slammed a fist into the captain's nose, leaving it bloody.

"Oi Nasim! Come, beat him up," Norden said, standing behind the captain and pinning his arms.

Nasim finally gathered courage. Taking a running start, he planted his left foot firmly on the ground and swung a kick at captain Garjé's shoulder with his right leg. He said, "Did you see my running kick?"

The captain didn't fall, but Nasim himself nearly did!

"Don't ever touch my boys," Norden raised his finger at the captain as he gave him a final warning. Then he turned to Nasim and declared, "We may not get to study in a school, and that's okay. But we will not put up with any beatings. D'you understand, Nasim?"

*

"Oh no, what will happen tomorrow?"

The captain was on Nasim's mind throughout the namaaz. Garjé's face swam before his eyes. He held his breath and prayed, "Allah, may the school be closed from tomorrow. May there be a holiday at school until the captain forgets his beating."

Norden was not just Nasim's schoolmate, but also his best friend. There was a time when they both used to study in the same class. But Norden was dull at studies and was now already two classes behind Nasim.

Norden was an exceedingly simple boy when he lived in the village. He was studying in Class 2 when his father suddenly left.

There was nothing to eat at home. He reached the village of Nimbong early morning one day, carrying a broom. It was there that he coincidentally met Raju-sir, who was in the village for a building contract job. He left for Kalimpong town along with Raju-sir, more out of the temptation of good food than to study. After he came to the town, its ways ensnared him. He started to become involved in delinquencies. Chunilal Chhetri of Aafate, who had come along with him, used to board with Aruna-miss and attend school in town. He wasn't any less delinquent either. Miss's house was near the Motor Stand. Perhaps that was why the ways of the bazaar had caught up with him. He used to smoke ganja now and then. He would climb onto the roofs of buses and chew on the chhurpi—dried hard cheese—he had stolen.

Norden was exceptional at drawing. He could sketch perfect figures. He might pick up a charcoal and get Lord Buddha to sit on a wall with his legs crossed. He might use a pencil to draw a sleepy Ganesh, trunk sprouting from his face. Sometimes he would make Goddess Laxmi sit with her legs crossed and laugh. At other times he would keep drawing Hanuman's face, muttering, "It's difficult to draw his face."

After he moved to town, he had to study in Class 2 again. Then he remained in Class 3 for two years as he didn't sit for the exams. Finally, Raju-sir promoted him to Class 4. That year, the school was celebrating its silver jubilee. He got a chance to dance to the song *Khanchhi hai kanchhi* and did so wonderfully. Sir was elated. Because of that dance, he was promoted to Class 5 without even appearing for the exams. He would be promoted just like that: sometimes by playing football well and sometimes by supplying jaand—millet beer—to Sir. He had not appeared for the previous year's exam either.

The school captain wielded as much power as the teachers. "If the news of the captain's beating reaches the school, we will get roasted alive," Nasim thought. He ran to the house where Norden lived.

The two-storey house was right below the bazaar. It stood next to a footpath after two bends on the road from town. Norden lived in a small room on its second floor with Raju-sir. There was not a single wall in that cramped house that was not covered with Norden's drawings.

Nasim walked down to the footpath and climbed up to the room. Just when he was about to enter the room, he saw three pairs of slippers and stood still. He gathered himself and yelled, "Oi, Norden!"

"Aren't you Nasim?" Standing at the door, Raju-sir asked in a soft voice.

Nasim stopped again. He blurted, "Namaste, Sir."

"Why greet me with a namaste in the evening?" Sir smiled a little. He ushered Nasim into the room and made him sit at a table.

Nasim was surprised. It was the first time that he had received such respect from his teacher.

There were two unfamiliar men in the room. Norden was sitting in a corner. Smiling, Norden beckoned Nasim and whispered into his ear, "They are talking about dangerous things here. They are talking about a revolution."

"A revolution?" Nasim tried to understand.

But it was not something he could comprehend. He kept thinking.

Nasim couldn't utter a word in front of his teacher. Raju-sir had been teaching him math since Class 5. It was difficult to speak to a teacher who taught a complicated subject.

"They are killing people in Darjeeling and Kurseong. They arrested fifty people in Kurseong yesterday too," Raju-sir started to talk. He was involved with the Gorkha Rashtriya Mukti Morcha (GORAMUMO), the Gorkha National Liberation Front. "Oppression has crossed all limits. Men must come forth from every home. To die for Gorkhaland is a matter of great fortune. The demonstration on the twenty-seventh will be amazing, just you wait and watch."

Nasim looked at Norden. Norden glued himself to Nasim's ear and whispered, "We won't pick a fight with other boys from now on. We will fight against the CPI(M) instead. If push comes to shove, we will take up arms as well. Sir has given us permission to do that, got it?"

"Guns?" Nasim was entranced. He really liked guns. He wanted to join the army so that he could fire them. As it turned out, one didn't necessarily have to join the army to fire guns. One could just as well join a revolution.

Nasim placed his chin on Norden's shoulder and said, "I will run away from home if you're joining the revolution."

"No, you don't have to run away just yet. We have posters. You can help us by putting them up," said Raju-sir, taking out some posters from his bag and laughing. "School is off tomorrow as well. Our protest on the twenty-seventh must be led by students. You can start work right away."

Norden first felt the posters and smelled them. He then said, "I will put all of them up today, for our own land!"

Nasim carried the posters without saying anything and followed Norden. He had no fear, for Norden was by his side.

There were just four of them when they reached the road. Two more boys joined them after they waited for ten minutes. They had brought homemade glue, which they used to quickly paste the posters on the walls.

They had put up only three posters when someone shouted at them, "Oi thieves! What are you doing?"

Everyone turned and looked up. A torchlight was switched on. It was the ward commissioner.

"You'll know what's what when the police give you kicks on your backsides!" the commissioner shouted, flashing the torchlight at them.

Norden nervously swallowed the spit in his mouth and blurted, borrowing Raju-sir's words, "We are ready to give up our lives for our land. Let the police come."

The police?

A nervous Nasim picked up Norden's bag and slowly made his way downhill.

Dhara 144

A N ant can carry a load twenty times its weight. To be small is not to be weak.

So what if their bodies were puny? Norden and Nasim had enough energy to touch the sky. Their dream was to scale mountains. To accomplish that, wouldn't they have to tread the path of a little pain?

The day after they put up the posters, Norden declared that he wasn't going to school anymore. How could Nasim have gone? After all, they had beaten up the school captain. He did one better and declared that he would not even go home. Every night in his dreams, he would run like the hero of *Rambo*, carrying a gun. That was why he would be with Norden day and night.

The first programme to be conducted by GORAMUMO was declared after three days. It was easy. They had to get the less-indoctrinated among the CPI(M) cadres to surrender. Thereafter, they were to travel from one village to another, selling calendars and secretly gathering information. They were to also tell people about the revolution.

The first programme was in Kalimpong town, in the Bhalukhop area. About twelve people were surrendering. It was said that one of them was resisting. That was why a new hero had come to lead the group. The boys called him Surya-da. Surya took on the responsibility of beating up the CPI(M) cadres.

Surya was thin. His hair was long. His eyes were slit-like and his face was always flushed. In fact, he was as hot-tempered as his name suggested.

"The only thing that is cold about me is my surname. I am a Rai, understood, a Rai!" he would declare. "From now on, I will personally heat up whosoever calls the Rai a cold-tempered people."

Surya was on his way to Bhalukhop. Norden and Nasim were walking behind him. Half a dozen boys were trailing behind.

Surya lit a beedi and puffed on it. He said, "We don't have our own land because of the CPI(M). You must have heard Budo's speech on the cassette the other day. What will you do if you run into a snake and a CPI(M) member?"

What a difficult question! Nasim froze. He hadn't listened to the cassette. And why would Norden care about it? Both of them stayed sheepishly quiet.

A reed-thin boy came forward, thrust a fist into the air and said, "I will kill the CPI(M) member first, and then the snake!"

"Are we going there to get people to surrender or to kill them?" Nasim thought. His legs grew weak. His eyes blurred. An icy fear gripped his heart. Yet he had some courage left in him. Gathering it, he asked, "What if the enemies don't agree to surrender, Surya-da?"

"I will kick the bastards." Surya turned around sharply. He swiped at the weeds growing by the roadside and said, "And you land them the second kick. How dare those devils not surrender!"

Nasim wilted. The boys set off downhill.

It was eleven when they reached Bhalukhop. Surya was walking ahead. Seeing Surya, a CPI(M) member came forward, looking as pitiful as a snake that has been struck on the head. He said, "Sir, we are ready. But maybe the flags won't be enough."

The villagers had gathered at the lower end of the village. They were now used to considering the Reds as the sinners and the Greens as the saints. Everyone was ready to become green.

"Where is your leader?" Surya flared up again. "I don't see him."

The comrade who was towards the front of the group was frightened by the loud voice. Out of fear, he nearly gave Surya the

Lal Salaam, the Red Salute. He checked himself and said, "He says he will leave home but not shun his ideology. That's why he fled to Siliguri."

"Your mother's . . . ! Who cares about ideology in a revolution?" Surya kicked at a wooden chair. The pathetic comrade stared at Surya.

GORAMUMO was getting stronger in the hills. GORAMUMO, the party demanding for Gorkhaland. This meant that anyone not part of GORAMUMO was someone who did not want Gorkhaland. That was how it was. And to be a Leftist was to be someone who was actively opposed to Gorkhaland, because the CPI(M) was the ruling party in government.

The revolutionaries would go to the villages and threaten the cadres of other parties into carrying their green flags. Those who did not comply became dissenters against the community. And becoming a dissenter was like requesting for your house to be set on fire. Your life would be in danger. Wouldn't it be better to run away than to take such a risk? That was why the CPI(M) leader had fled to Himali Nagar in Siliguri.

The comrade thought of the old leader for a long time and then said, "You are our leader now and you have our support. Our understanding was wrong all this time. Please forgive us."

No one knew if Surya understood. However, a new surya, a new sun, had dawned upon his face, which everyone noticed.

A green flag was added to each hand present then and there. And all the Reds turned Green from that day on, except for the leader whom Surya had enquired about.

On their way back, Surya proudly announced a new plan, "We have to distribute the calendars from tomorrow. Understood, boys?"

The night passed uneventfully.

Early the following morning, Surya took a bundle of calendars and decreed, "Raju-sir has told us to sell these. Nasim, Norden, and I will take care of it. The rest will stay here and help Raju-sir. Do you understand, boys?"

The calendar had a large picture of Subhash Ghising on it.

The reed-thin boy who had said that he would first kill the CPI(M) and then the snake came forward, saying "Yes Sir!" and leaving the room.

Nasim had wanted to say, "No, I will not go," but not a word came out of his mouth. He picked up a calendar, scratched his head and asked, "Surya-da, why is this revolution happening?"

"I'm not sure why." Surya fell silent for a while. He then wrinkled his forehead, thought about something and said, "This revolution is for the land. There is a protest march this week. Got it?"

"What is a protest march?"

"Jaantha! Do what you have been told to do. Are you a leader who needs to understand everything?"

The calendar was now in everyone's hands. Nasim walked silently down to Dungra village. Norden headed off to Algarah to the south of Kalimpong and Surya to Pudung in the east.

It was not difficult to sell the calendars. They met gentlefolk in the villages. All they had to do was pass on the information and the villagers would be ready to participate. As they sold the calendars, they would speak about the protest march to be held on the 27th of July. Three days passed like that.

It was in the evening on the fourth day that Surya heard the news broadcast by Akashvani Kurseong: "Five people were killed in Kurseong. Fifty-five were arrested in Darjeeling."

His heart sank. Before splitting up, the three of them had agreed to meet on the crossroads at Pudung before sundown on the fourth day. He thought of Norden and Nasim. Fixing a wad of chewing tobacco behind his lip, he set off uphill.

"The people in the villages are very good." A new thought swirled in Surya's mind on his way back. "Damn, they respect even people like us. They honour us like they would honour leaders. They give us whatever they've cooked at home! They buy our calendars even with the money they've offered to the gods. If things stay like this, we'll definitely get our land."

He paused for a moment to think. Then he felt the coins in his pocket and started to walk rapidly up the hilly path leading to the crossroads in Pudung.

"Surya-da, we've arrived here much earlier." Nasim said ingratiatingly as soon as he saw him. "And we were waiting for you, Da."

Norden smiled at Nasim's words.

Surya started to brag. "You can't have walked as much as I did. Look down there. I walked over that entire hillside."

The forest was alive with susurrations. There was a spring by the wayside and a waterspout that channelled water from it. The water splashed loudly on the ground. They drank some of it and walked on. Another uphill walk began over the slopes of Pudung hill. They had to reach Rausey the next day and attend the protest. The grandeur of the revolution finally dawned on Nasim.

"They say many people have died in Darjeeling," Norden said, turning his face towards the setting sun. "There's a lot of talk in the villages. The government has humiliated us for far too long. We should not put up with it now. Understand?"

Nasim nodded his head without understanding.

"Once Chief builds the guns," Surya said, making a new revelation, "I will be the first one to shoot the syarpi[9]."

For both Nasim and Norden, this was a revelation.

"Who is our chief? Raju-sir?" Nasim asked, scratching his head.

Surya laughed theatrically. There was a wormwood bush by the path. He caught hold of it, plucked a bud and put it in his mouth. Pretending that it wasn't bitter, he said, "Chief is Chief. I will point him out to you tomorrow. Raju-sir is ranked below Chief and I am below Sir, got it?"

---

[9] Local slang for the Central Reserve Police Force (CRPF).

Having ranked himself below Raju-sir, Surya fell silent for some time. He watched Nasim's face. Perhaps he wanted to see the faith Nasim had in him. He may have seen it, or perhaps not. He walked on.

Dusk set in when they were still climbing. Night fell. Now they were in trouble. Nothing was visible. There weren't any houses nearby either. When they had walked for half an hour, they realised that they had taken the wrong path and reached 14th Mile. Surya sank to the ground. Out of all of them he had walked the most and was very tired.

"There is a house." After they had rested for a while, Nasim pointed out a light coming from a wick-lamp.

Luckily it *was* a house, though it was built like a cowshed. Plucking another bud off a wormwood bush, the three walked up to it. Surya made Nasim walk ahead. The house owner was more likely to open the door if she saw a kid, and that was what happened.

Boju, the old woman, was alone at home. Her son had gone away to be a part of the revolution.

"Boju, we are also revolutionaries," Norden swaggered. "We spent two days in the Paari hills. Night fell as we were returning today. Will you give us a place to stay here?"

Boju coughed for some time. Her face wrinkled further. She thought for a second and said, "Sure. You can eat what I have cooked. But it is dark as they have cut off the electricity. Maybe it will be difficult for you, sons."

"Why did they cut off the electricity?" Nasim asked in a low voice. "This place is quite near the bazaar. There is electricity in that house there."

"That Rajen-sir cut the supply, saying I don't have the proper papers," said Boju.

"I will meet him tomorrow. Who cares about papers in a revolution? Did you say that his name is Rajen?" Surya's temper immediately ran high.

Then came the sound of people walking on the path above the house. Boju put her ear to the window. A group of people were heading towards town.

As the sound of the footsteps receded, Boju gave them water to drink. She then uncovered a cooking pot and gave them four pieces of steamed chayote.

The three were tired. Even more, they were hungry. They gobbled up the chayote and fell asleep.

Nasim was the first to get up in the morning. He woke Norden up and then Surya. Surya stretched, turning towards the rising sun and said, "Let us go to Raju-sir's home today. We have to hand over the money from the sale of the calendars. We will walk down to Rausey in the evening. Chief's house is there."

Nasim pretended to think for a while. He then looked up. His house was somewhere in the neighbourhood. He wondered if he should go home. But he didn't have the courage to do that yet. It had been a week since he had run away. More importantly, the revolution was an attraction. It was the dream of playing with guns. What was there at home? What else besides reading the namaaz? He followed Surya.

Their excitement grew as they reached the bazaar. After all, it was their own stomping ground. Green flags were going up all around town. It looked splendid.

They had also put up a big welcome gate just below the electricity office, which reminded Nasim of the old woman they had met the day before.

"Surya-da, are we meeting Rajen-sir?" Nasim asked.

"Ay, we need to." Surya grew heated, but his excitement dampened when he saw that the electricity office was nearby. He said, "Let's tell him once. If this work is done, at least we will have done some dharma."

The three walked up the steps to the office.

"Who is Rajen-sir?" Surya asked, standing at the door.

Rajen-sir hadn't arrived yet. The office gates have just been opened. Sir hardly arrives this early.

"He is the same sir who cut off the electricity in Topkhana the other day in Boju's house, y'know?" The gatekeeper looked terrified when he heard Surya say this, but he kept mum.

"Which Boju?" For a while, the gatekeeper pretended to think of Boju.

"Let's go, he's not here," Norden said, standing beside him.

The three of them came back to the road and headed towards Raju-sir's home. There were many boys there. They handed him the money.

"You just wait and see, people will swarm like ants on the twenty-seventh," Surya bragged again.

The boys then ate some roti and lay down on the floor. Norden picked up a piece of charcoal and started to draw on the wall. In the sketch, there was a huge crowd of people.

Raju-sir seemed to be busy most of the day. Sometimes, he seemed to be writing or thinking of something. Nasim faced west and sat listlessly.

They spent the day this way. Come evening, they were ready to return.

"They won't arrest us if we go through the bazaar, will they?" Nasim's feeble voice quivered. "They say it is full of syarpis because of the protest tomorrow."

"What will those fuckers do, huh?" Surya cried. "They're just like us. They are here to do their duty. And we are here for the revolution. Got it?"

They were to go through the bazaar.

The banyan and peepal trees were standing tall in front of Thana Dara, where the Kalimpong Police Station was situated. Surya stood there for a couple of minutes and said, "We will win if there are no additional syarpis tomorrow."

"What will we win?" Nasim was perplexed. He then looked towards the town. Awestruck by what he saw, he exclaimed, "Baaf re, the town has become green!"

Green flags had been put up everywhere. The newly-built gates were green. Even the festoons were green. To top it all, the forests surrounding the town were green too. By god, it looked as if the whole world was green, completely green!

The three headed down to Rausey, just outside of town where a camp of the Gorkha Volunteer Cell (GVC) had been set up.

"Bloody hell! They have finally arrived! I hope you did your work well." Chief was in the camp. On his head was a huge, felted hat. He turned his head towards the boys. The felted hat turned along with his head. He then closed his eyes and cried, "Make sure that people don't get frightened and stay home tomorrow!"

"Bloody hell?" Something was cooking in Nasim's head. Norden smiled. Surya stood behind Chief.

Chief was about to say something when Raju-sir came to the meeting room. He handed over a report. Then he showed Chief the sales statement of the calendars. Others had also gathered. The sun set and night advanced. The meeting began.

Chief narrated the plan, "The people from Labha, Kagey, Algarah and Pedong will come via 10th Mile. You boy, what's your name? Yes, Norden. You keep watch there. You don't have to do anything. Just make sure the people walk in a line. You don't have to even walk with them."

"People from East Main Road and Bong Basti will all emerge together near the post office. Those are our core areas. Surya, you will handle them. But don't get cocky and mess up the job!

"People from Peshok and the Teesta highway will enter from 8th Mile. You, what's your name? You will stay there. Have you understood?"

Nasim's eyes darted towards Chief. He coughed a little. "My name is Nasim, Chief."

"You are a student, aren't you?"

"Yes, Chief."

"Students are the face of tomorrow's protest. The bloody police may try to stop you. You mustn't be scared, got it?"

Nasim nodded, only half understanding what Chief said.

"The rest of you boys come with me. All of you must reach Mela Ground at noon. All the party heads will be there. The main treaty-burning programme will be held on the ground. Understood, boys?"

Everyone looked at each other's faces. Nasim had turned pale and a chill ran down Norden's spine. But both of them felt relieved upon seeing Surya's face. They had all been given responsibilities and all of them understood their positions. They exited the camp.

"Surya, a Boju has come to meet you," someone called out from inside the room. Surya's face briefly lit up with anger. He went outside. Norden and Nasim followed him.

It was the same old woman they had met yesterday. A new tension had now been added. Why was she here?

"What happened, Boju?" Surya pulled her to a corner and asked, lowering his voice.

Boju's face brightened. Showing her teeth, she said, "Thank you, son! May my blessings do you good, the power is on at home."

Nasim was mystified.

"What did Rajen-sir say?" Surya asked, relieved.

Boju coughed a little and said, "He was afraid. He said I need not have sent the sirs from Rausey to the office. Thieving bastard!"

"You go back home," Surya said, smiling. "Why did you come here?"

"Oh, I heard that Dhara 144 has been enforced in the bazaar," Boju said, coughing. "We face water shortages too. You young ones saw how bad things were yesterday. So I was wondering if we could get a dhara[10] too. Please do this pious act. My blessings will always be with you."

Surya lost it. Stamping his foot, he said, "Whatever else may be

[10] "Dhara" can refer to sections of the Indian Constitution as well as sources of water, either underground springs or flowing brooks that have been channelized to provide drinking water or irrigation.

going on in the house, the son-in-law is concerned only with his meals! You're like that. You don't understand anything. Now go home and stay there quietly."

Silence spread over the courtyard. Boju went on her way. Surya asked himself, "Is this Dhara 144 actually a waterspout? Was that why she was asking?"

Black Day

A little sunshine. A little cloud. A little excitement. A little disappointment. Sunday arrived, bearing everything aloft.

Sleep left Nasim before 4 a.m. A new dream dawned before his eyes. The plans and schemes of the protest kept roiling in his mind. Norden was also awake. He rolled over and woke Surya up. Surya stretched and turned to the east. Raju-sir was already busy writing something.

"Something is not quite right today," Nasim said, turning to Norden.

"One day one thing is not quite right, on another day something else isn't," Raju-sir said, looking up from the register in which he was writing. "Life is made up of contradictions, of the coming together of the things that are not quite right."

Surya laced up his worn-out boots while sitting on the bed and ran off towards the playground. Nasim and Norden followed him. They returned after running two circuits.

*

Raju-sir was standing a little to the front. The heavily bearded, middle-aged NB-sir was standing at his side. The secretary of the party's Kalimpong district chapter, NB-sir, wore his hair long. He had on a leather jacket and an old pair of gloves. The gloves were torn in the middle and one could clearly see his palms.

NB-sir went over the plan that had been shared with them the previous day. "I am saying this to you as the party secretary, this is a fight for our soil. You should not hesitate even if it means sacrificing your life. Do you get it, boys?"

The day was foggy. Every time he spoke, vapour would blow out of NB-sir's mouth. He shouted at the end, exhaling a billow of vapour, "Jai Gorkha!"

Everyone repeated the slogan after him. It uplifted the whole camp.

The boys got pumped up.

"Should I carry a khukuri?" Norden asked, pointlessly.

"Can you cut down the syarpis?" Surya doubted Norden's capability. Still, he winked and said, "Of course you should carry one, you donkey! Carry it discreetly, like this."

Aaloo kaati tarkaari taama lai, na chalaunu Ghorkali aama lai. Applying green tika on the boys' foreheads, Surya asked "Have you heard this song? We must sing this at the protest, boys."

Nasim hadn't heard the song before. Yet he nodded and smiled.

A level road went from the camp to a chautari, a resting place under a tree. The locality of Joredhara was to the right of the chautari. They reached Rachela's house as soon as they climbed the road up to Joredhara.

Rachela?

Nasim's classmate Rachela Pradhan would frequently pay him visits in his dreams.

Raju-sir used to say, "Rachela is good at her studies." But Nasim used to think, "Rachela is good at everything. Everything."

Rachela was doing the dishes. Seeing Nasim, she smiled softly and asked, "Where are you going, Nasim?"

Nasim was no longer the Nasim who had taken a beating at school. He had turned into a different individual.

Raju-sir would say, "Revolutionaries must be like matchsticks. Always walking with gunpowder inside their heads, always ready to explode."

Nasim really liked this line. Inspired by it, he said, "The entire hills are burning. But you, Pradhan girl, you stay here okay, washing dishes!"

Wah! What beautiful words. And they had come straight out of his own mouth! He was delighted. Surya turned around to look at him.

Nasim continued, "I had heard that the Pradhans are penny-pinchers. Are they also cowards?"

Norden smirked.

Nasim looked into Rachela's eyes for a long time.

"Everyone in the house has gone to the protest. But this really is too much. Wait, I will also come. Okay?" Rachela put aside the dishes.

"We have duties to attend to there. You go with the other people, alright?" Overwhelmed by his emotions, Nasim ran after Surya.

"Duty." This word had puffed up Nasim's chest and put a new swagger in his step.

The town was colourful. The three split up when they neared Haat Bazaar. Nasim's legs trembled a little. His face turned pale. His voice seemed to have stuck in his throat. Still, he said, coughing, "We will meet in the evening, boys, won't we?"

"Hyah! This Muslim is such a sissy," Surya spat out the tobacco he was chewing and continued, "Weren't you talking big in front of that Pradhan girl earlier?"

Nasim went limp and slowly set off uphill. Surya left for Saatdobato. Norden walked off towards 10th Mile. Shaking in fear, Nasim passed by the police station and headed to 8th Mile.

The day was overcast. It seemed like the sun would vanish behind the clouds. The clock was about to strike eleven.

The crowd quickly swelled. Most of the people were dressed in the traditional daura-suruwal. Everyone was singing and dancing. Those who had smeared green paint all over their bodies were surging forward, jumping.

Nasim finally plucked up some courage. He ordered the line

to move forward and commanded, "Put the students up in front. That's the president's order!"

Notwithstanding the pushing and shoving, an orderly line was formed. Those who were in front did not come towards the rear. The students remained at the back and started shouting slogans. God, what excitement!

As more people joined the crowd, its contours changed. It took on a new countenance.

Suddenly, a loud sound could be heard. The police immediately raised their shields. Those wielding guns formed a line. The marchers stopped abruptly at Engine Dara just outside town.

A police officer was chewing paan. Someone brought a small hand-mic and gave it to him. Speaking in Hindi, he shouted into the mic, "You cannot all go ahead together. Dhara 144 has been imposed from here on!"

The crowd milled about in the same spot and started to shout slogans.

Nasim did not know what to do. They had to reach Mela Ground. He came up with an idea and ordered the ladies to be at the head of the procession. He was certain that those who were in the front would make way for them.

But it didn't work. The protestors did not agree to give up their places. The policemen remained firm as a wall.

The front ranks turned around and came to the rear. People coming from other places must have already reached Mela Ground. Nasim's tension increased. Just then, another group came shouting from behind them. The man leading the group was in great excitement. He was tall and wore a headband. As soon as he saw the police, he started hurling abuse.

He must have been a little drunk. He turned to the protesters and shouted:

"We Gorkhas won't obey the syarpis. Won't obey! Won't obey! Break this barricade, boys!"

He advanced. The group following him also moved forward. The police officer shouted a warning, but the tall man ignored it. Nasim turned towards the back and kept standing still. The police tried to stop the leader again. He wouldn't listen. He kept surging forward.

The situation became tense. The tall man still refused to heed the warnings. He started arguing with the police. He ran about, swinging an unsheathed khukuri in the air. The revolutionaries started jumping and shouting a war cry: *Jai jai Kali Mahakali, aayo aayo Ghorkali!* (Hail hail Great Goddess Kali, here we come, here we come, we Gorkhali!)

The police officer couldn't bear it any longer. He started to yell even more loudly into the mic.

The police started to fire tear gas at the demonstrators. Surprisingly, the tall man disappeared from the line of protestors. A boy had been standing right behind him. He had eyes like slits. His hair was unkempt. He had a tiny dream on his face. It was that dream that prevented him from fleeing.

This boy advanced, picked up a tear-gas shell, and threw it towards the police where it exploded. The police were upwind of the fumes, which made it even more difficult for them to stand their ground.

And then?

The police officer bellowed one last time. No one could understand anything.

Something that no one had expected happened. All at once, the sound of guns could be heard. People started to fall. The slit-eyed boy plunged into a gutter. Those who were at the back began to run. Nasim ran too, jumping into the gutter to save himself. The revolutionaries dispersed at once.

A thick-set man came forward. He had an old Commander jeep. Parking the jeep by the side of the road, he walked up to the police with his hands folded in supplication. He sought their permission to pick up those who had fallen.

Nobody could figure out what that man who spoke in a Tibetan accent said to the police officer, but the force stepped back. He started to carry the injured to his jeep.

Nasim finally reappeared on the road. His legs were still trembling and his eyes were in a haze.

Seeing Nasim, the Tibetan man gestured to him and said, "Oi you boy, see all who have fallen here? Put them in the jeep. We need to take them to the hospital, or they will die."

Nasim looked into the gutter. The slit-eyed boy was lying down there, drenched in blood. Nasim carried him on his shoulder and put him in the jeep. The jeep sped off to the hospital.

*

"There is news of police firing at 8th Mile." This information gradually reached Damber Chowk. It then reached Saatdobato. And then 10th Mile, where the revolutionaries had been stopped by the police. The sloganeers instantly grew angry. They broke down the police barricades and slowly marched north towards Thana Dara. The revolutionaries starting out from East Main Road, just beyond the centre of town, had already come near Thana Dara. Their dancing continued unabated.

The revolutionaries were still cheerful. They carried the dream of a separate homeland in their eyes.

At Thana Dara, the CRPF had put up another barricade. They were shouting from the police station above the road, repeating that Dhara 144 had been imposed. People were busy dancing and singing. Armed to the teeth, the police were standing in front of them like a wall. Still, the people weren't willing to retreat. Slogans kept resounding. Clenched fists remained raised towards the sky.

"They're saying that those hit by the bullets are unlikely to survive." Another rumour slipped into the crowd. People started shouting even more loudly. Their rage rose. At that instant, one of the men in uniform shouted, "We will not spare anyone who assaults the police."

The noise in the street suddenly shot up. A loud sound came from somewhere. Nobody had time to think as shots were fired.

"Look! The taekwondo master has come," someone cried out.

A tall boy came running down the road, an unsheathed khukuri clenched between his teeth. As he reached the Chowk, he swung a leg. He brandished the khukuri. A syarpi fell down in a heap.

He hadn't got up yet when a woman standing a little ahead of him drew a sickle and sank it into the chest of another syarpi. The woman hadn't even had time to turn around when they heard the sound of gunfire.

Taekwondo master and sickle fell on the same spot.

Disaster had struck.

Darkness descended over Kalimpong. People ran helter-skelter to save their lives. Those who were hit fell wherever they were standing. The women started to cry. The men started to run towards the jungles. There was complete darkness.

Nearly ten minutes passed just like that. The din quieted down slowly. The gun-carrying policemen retreated. The situation normalised a little. Just then, a familiar jeep arrived, and Nasim and Norden too appeared.

Those who were in the jeep started to pick up the fallen. They did not have the courage to look at their faces, so they would put them in the vehicle as quickly as they could and then pick up the others.

It was only after the jeep had made two trips to the hospital that Norden's eyes clouded over. The entire road had turned black. Everything was slathered in blood. The hundreds of slippers lying around were the lone revolutionaries standing in protest. The road was utterly deserted. There was no one except the wounded and those helping the wounded.

"Oi Nasim! Look here, Rachela is also wounded," Norden stuttered nervously.

Nasim turned towards Norden. He saw Rachela. The same Rachela whom he had goaded to join the demonstration. That same Rachela of his dreams who could make him forget Allah.

Nasim froze. No sound could emerge from his mouth. The tears did not roll down his cheeks. He picked up Rachela and put her into the jeep, wrapping her in a cloth. Her insides were spilling out of her abdomen. She was in no condition to speak.

Rachela was taken to the hospital. There wasn't any space for new patients, and it was going to take time to arrange a bed for her. Nasim raised Rachela up slowly and placed her head on his lap. He gave her some water to drink and sprinkled some of it on her head. Rachela heaved a long sigh and said in a faint voice, "I will live, won't I Nasim?" Rachela's voice was quavering. Tears and splotches of blood blackened her face.

She tried to say more but couldn't. Only her lips trembled.

Nasim too was soaked in blood. He looked at her face reluctantly and said, "I made a great mistake by asking you to come to the demonstration, didn't I?"

Rachela moved her lips again. But not a word emerged. Tears streamed from her eyes.

All of a sudden, Rachela's eyes closed. Her hands lolled downwards towards the earth. The soles of her feet turned upward.

Standing near Rachela's corpse, Nasim began to sob.

*

Nasim and Norden arrived in Rausey in the evening, but Nasim fainted before they could enter the camp. He remained unconscious for three hours. He did not speak or drink a drop of water. His eyes could see no light. Everything was dark. Pitch dark.

He finally regained consciousness at around 7 p.m. Akashvani was broadcasting the news: "The CRPF opened fire in Kalimpong. Thirteen agitators were killed."

On the following day, the BBC announced that it was a "Black Sunday" for Darjeeling.

That indeed was the blackest day for Darjeeling.

THE ATTACK

FIFTEEN days passed by just like that.

Nasim remained in mourning. The boys would bring him raksi. He would force it down his throat and sit staring towards the west.

Surya would drink raksi from early morning. He would sharpen his khukuri, then put it back into its scabbard. There was a needlewood tree near the camp. He would go punch it, then come sit near Nasim and take drags on a beedi. Norden would pick up a piece of charcoal and draw a picture of Hanuman on the ground, saying, "It is difficult to draw the cheeks of this god." He would erase the head, add the trunk of an elephant, and say, "Ganesh-ji, please give me strength," while putting his hands together.

The camp was silent. The wind would blow in gusts, as if it were angry. The sun would emerge coyly before slipping quickly behind the clouds.

"It will take twenty-one days. And then everything will change. Don't worry," Raju-sir said. "After twenty days, you will become men who drink not just alcohol, but also human blood. Get it?"

Norden was amazed. Still tipsy, Surya asked curtly, "Which magician will come in twenty-one days to cure him with his wizardry?"

"It takes twenty-one days for a person to change. Try doing anything for twenty-one days, it will become a habit." He then walked out of the room.

Hogwash. Norden didn't believe him. Even so, he counted his fingers. Looking into Nasim's eyes, he said, "What Sir said must be true. Nasim, you will remain like this for six more days."

Nasim was facing west. The clouds on his face hadn't cleared. Norden grinned and repeated what he had said earlier, "It will take twenty-one days for you to recover. After that, we won't drink alcohol but blood, you hear, blood!"

"Rachela has called me to her." These words escaped Nasim's mouth. He clenched his fists and teeth and cried, "I will go where Rachela is."

Evening was falling.

The hills were shut down. A shadow fell over Norden's face.

Surya came running back into the camp.

The revolution had become about felling trees. People fell trees and lay them across the roads to obstruct the vehicles used by the CRPF.

The others who had also gone out to fell trees had returned. A sizable crowd gathered around Nasim.

"Shit, has he gone crazy?" Norden said softly.

A fire had been set alight right behind the camp. Some boys were roasting banana blossoms in the fire. A thin boy came, handed them a dirty kettle, and left. The kettle went from hand to hand and from mouth to mouth.

Norden felt Nasim's forehead and said, "I don't think he can hold out for long. Let's send him home."

Surya was puffing on a beedi. He passed the beedi butt to Norden and thought for a while, staring at the sky. Norden puffed at it and turned to Nasim.

"There are shamans in the forest of Rachela. They abduct children. Has a shaman cast a spell on him?" a shaggy-haired boy who was roasting banana blossoms asked. "Why does he want to go to Rachela all at once? Give him a drink from the kettle."

"Don't talk rubbish." Norden threw away the butt and looked into Surya's eyes with dejection. In those eyes he saw Nasim's father with a scarf tied around his head, waiting for his beloved son.

"Maybe we should do that," Surya said, after thinking things over for a while. "I will have one less boy, but he might die if he stays here. Let's take him home."

Norden nodded. Just then, the kettle fell on the floor with a clatter. Someone kicked it and it rolled some distance before stopping.

The kettle had just stopped clattering when the camp rang out with loud cries.

People began to scream. The silent evening filled up with noise. Everyone got up and started to run helter-skelter. The din was intense, as though all the trembling voices were filling up an echo chamber. Everything was shaking up.

"Kill them . . . ! Kill them . . . !" A mob of boys rushed in through the main entrance of the camp. Everyone darted when they saw the boys running in with their faces covered. Nasim didn't move an inch.

Norden turned pale with fright. When the mind doesn't function properly, you forget to run. That was what happened to Norden.

Surya was heading downhill when his foot hit the kettle. His gumboot slipped off and he took a tumble over two terraced fields. All the boys scattered.

They all had a single thought. They should not all run in the same direction but make sure to go different ways. Their pursuers would be confused by this tactic.

"Has our time come?" This thought ran through Norden's mind as he turned around and ran off. What would come, would come. His eyes were still closed.

Just then, a loud voice rang out, "Bloody fools! Is this how you were trained?"

Only then did the boys open their eyes. Standing in front of them was the Chief, wearing the felted hat. His eyes were scrunched up in rage.

"You sons of pigs!" He clenched his fists. He then turned to Surya and shouted, "You donkeys, is this your training? Will you run away like this if the enemy attacks?"

Surya's eyes rolled in fear. He picked up his gumboot and stood at attention, "Forgive us, Chief."

Surya brought his trembling legs under control.

"Turns out there is nothing better than being alive," he said to himself and put on the gumboot.

"Will sheep like these ever drive the revolution?" Chief asked, now calmer. "Is this what they mean when they say that the Gorkhalis don't run from battle? You will die fleeing, not fighting."

The boys became alert. "Sorry, Chief," Surya said, mustering courage. "We were all tense because of the other day. Our minds didn't work when we were suddenly attacked."

"Where is Norden?" Chief asked, coming forward.

"I am here, Chief," Norden's voice quavered.

"Do you know how to use a khukuri?"

Did a word escape Norden's mouth? There was only the sound of his breath as he exhaled. Chief started to swing his khukuri about. Only the swish of the blade was in the air.

"Surya and you, help this sir here. We have to make guns now," Chief's finger was wagging in front of Nasim's face. A middle-aged man with a crewcut was standing beside Chief.

A voice emerged from Nasim's mouth after many days: "Yes, Sir."

"Say Chief, not sir," Norden scolded him. He added, "You fucker! You have become insensate out of fear. Now that same fear has made you well again."

Chief went off into his room, smiling.

Chief

MAN becomes powerful not because of his physique but because of his courage.

Hitler's victory over half the world was not because of his physical frame but his recklessness. Napoleon made history not because of his build but his bravery.

Like Hitler and Napoleon, Chief was short. His moustache was thick and grand, and he constantly wanted to twirl it. He always wore dingo boots. Their heels would sink right into the ground whenever he walked on mud. On his head was a felted hat, on which a small axe glinted. There was always a khukuri slung from his waist. He would take his khukuri out and swing it— swish, swish—in the air, and the boys would gape at the swinging khukuri, frightened.

He had always been stubborn since he was a child. The villagers called him Kalu. Kalu's record in fights was excellent. He had never lost a single one.

When he was in Class 3, he beat up a student from Class 9. Thereafter, he had more enemies than friends in school.

But his greatest enemies were always books. When Sharma-sir arrived, however, he became an even greater enemy than the books. Sharma-sir's eyes were so sharp that they would see everything the students did. He would pick up the wooden blackboard duster as he taught and hurl it at Kalu, who would be sitting on the last bench. Every time the duster bounced off his head, Kalu would think, "How does Sharma-sir see from behind his dark glasses?"

It was around this time that the annual examinations ended. Lepcha-sir had come to class to distribute report cards. Lepcha-sir was extremely gentle. If there was one teacher in school who did not hurl dusters at Kalu, it was Lepcha-sir. Whenever the students saw him, they would say, "Teachers should be like Lepcha-sir. Someone who never gets angry. After all, even the police know how to beat people up."

Kalu was eleven years old at that time. He had reached Class 3 without studying a thing! But it was going to be tough for him. The villagers would say, "It is very hard to pass Class 3."

Lepcha-sir had said something that Kalu had never thought about: "You too have passed."

Kalu was elated at first, but became furious at the next instant. He stood up, went up to Sir and said, "The 'you have passed' bit was fine. Why did you add 'too' in my case?"

"You pass only now and then. Otherwise, your failing is guaranteed," Lepcha-sir replied. "That's why I said what I said. Got it?"

The whole class burst into peals of laughter.

Kalu quietly picked up his report card and set off for Mela Ground.

Football fever was gripping Kalimpong. Others were also heading towards the ground. The tall and thin Khadke was leading a group of boys. He started speaking, "That Half-Pant Uncle plays superbly, doesn't he?"

The other boys agreed with him.

A pair of half-pants that had been cut out of full trousers. His big toe sticking out of a torn shoe. Scabs of snot sticking to his cheeks, and a little rheum in the corners of his eyes. Kalu suddenly turned around and punched Khadke, saying, "Why did you laugh when Sir said that I had passed?"

Khadke ran off home. The rest followed Kalu.

The Motor Stand was quite empty. They started watching the

game from there.

The match was exciting. None of the sides had scored a goal. A drunkard sitting on the wall at one of the sides of the ground was shouting. He started to dance. The boys goaded him on.

A group of girls from Kalimpong Girls' High School were sitting in the first row of the gallery; they climbed up the tiered seats to have a better view of the game. Pabitra Bhandari was among them. Of dusky complexion, she looked attractive in her school uniform. She walked towards Kalu and looked at him fixedly. And then, for some reason, she put a hand on her mouth, tittered, and ran up to the last row of seats.

Kalu only liked dusky girls, not fair ones. When Pabitra giggled, he forgot the game happening on the ground. He puffed up his chest and whispered to the boys sitting by his side, "Pabitra smiled at me today. Did you see her?"

"She didn't smile at you," Harichandra said, hesitating in fear. "Your half-pants are torn. Your thing is peeping out."

Thing!

Kalu turned fiery with anger. He ran home, his eyes shut in humiliation.

His mother was at home. He shouted from outside the house, "Aama, hand me the khukuri!"

Aama gave him the knife. He then took off his half-pants, put it on a block of wood and started chopping it up. This was his only pair. It was torn into seven pieces.

That day, he slept naked. He didn't go to school the next day. Lost in thought, he went to the jungle instead. He remained there all day, roasting and eating corn.

It was two days after this that he wore the first pair of trousers in his life.

And it was four years after he wore his first pair of trousers that he lied about his age and joined the army.

He had yet to start earning a salary in the army when he became fed up with the work. Who could control him when he is the master of his will? He returned home.

It was after he came back home that the village witnessed the festival of Dashain, which brought evil along that year.

*

Kalu's middle-aged father was standing near the marigold patch. He turned towards his son, spat and cursed, "You donkey! You've given up a good paying job! You've ruined Dashain."

"Does one have to create a spectacle at Dashain?" Kalu asked.

A friend came to his defence and said in a timid voice, "What could he do when he didn't like the job?"

A shadow came over his father's face. He reluctantly went off to the fields. He recalled the instant when his son had been born. How he had puffed up with pride when he joined the army. Then how he had deserted and come home as soon as training ended. His face fell.

Kalu was lost in his own thoughts. He clutched a millet stalk and watched his father leave.

His father had yet to reach the fields when the sun disappeared. The wind started to show its anger. The white clouds turned black and began to cry.

Father returned home without working the fields and stood under the eaves. He looked up at the sky and spat, "Damned luck! It is raining in the month of Asoj."

Night fell. Morning came. Then evening. Night fell again. The rain did not stop. Rice grains growing like gold nuggets on paddy plants fell to the ground. Millet stems keeled over in the direction that the wind blew them.

But was that enough? Two days later, one side of the fields was swept away by a landslide. A heap of sand spread over the place where the marigold flowers once stood.

The damned rain! It swept everything away. Most importantly, it swept away dreams. It engulfed people. It destroyed roads. It disfigured the face of Darjeeling.

After three days, three full days, the rain finally stopped. But what if it did stop? A new plight began thereafter.

Those whom the rain had spared were swept away by their tears.

Until three days ago, life had been beautiful, like a garland of marigold flowers. That garland was now torn into sixty-eight pieces. Only one number kept ricocheting in everyone's minds: "1968. This accursed year!"

And thereafter?

Those who survived memorised "68", the way one memorizes one's roll number in school.

Kalu's father never knew how to write the number "68". Neither could he recognise it. But the sentence: "Damned year '68! It ruined everything," stayed with him.

The villagers would sit with their heads in their hands and brood. They would look at the fields that had been swept away, sigh deeply and spit at the sky.

Five days after the landslide, Kalu's father suddenly became angry, "Mula! What will you eat now? Your father's banana?"

A dark cloud fell over Kalu's face. He despaired. He stood quietly for some time. Then he thought of something, opened his eyes, and took a deep breath. Staring at the sinking sun, he declared, "Whatever happens, I will join the army again."

His eyes finally met his father's. For the first time, he saw a small world of love in his father's eyes.

*

Name?

Chandra Singh Subba.

Father's name?

Lalbir Subba.

Address?

Dungra, Kalimpong.

Educational qualification?

The minimum required.

Two months after the landslide, Kalu became Chandra Singh—Soldier Chandra Singh.

The disfigured image of Darjeeling had yet to heal when Kalu went off to join the army. He wanted to first heal the wound festering in his father's heart.

Whenever he was drunk, Kalu's grandfather would say, "You will reach Nepal if you have brains, and Burma if you have brawn. It will be as it is written in the stars."

*

One day, he was taking part in a parade.

"Will you also box?" asked an officer, looking him in the eye.

"Ji Sir," Chandra Singh said, standing up on his toes and saluting smartly. He had finally found something in the army which he enjoyed. He could beat up people there too.

He spent nearly fourteen years beating people up. The boxing ring became his world.

One day something new happened. Something unthinkable. Chandra Singh lost his service book.

Other soldiers instilled fear in him, warning, "Punishment for losing one's service book is severe."

He lost his wits. His sleep vanished. His face fell. He was unable to focus on his boxing and began to spend his days in anxiety. Don't they say that even the sun seems hotter when one's in trouble? That was what happened.

The sun was scorching hot that day. Sitting in the shade, he was reading an English newspaper. A headline caught his attention:

"Ghising to Demand a Separate State for Darjeeling."

Nepalis were being chased away from north-eastern India. Everyone was already feeling insecure. Anger rose in him.

That same day, his village started to become a constant presence in his dreams again.

He declared to himself, "The land is calling out to me. I will return to Darjeeling. I will fight for our race."

In fact, the matter of the service book was also the source of tension in his mind.

Chandra Singh decided to leave the army for good and return to Darjeeling.

He was preparing his papers to return home when another surprising incident occurred. He found his lost service book. That damned thing had been in his coat pocket all along!

Binduli tika ke tika
Sindoor ko tika ke tika

Mato ko tika raja tika
Mato ko tika rani tika

That bindi on your forehead
Is that a tika?

The auspicious vermilion in the parting of your hair
Is that a tika?

The soil which anoints your brow
That is the king tika

The soil which adorns your forehead
That is the queen tika

"The time is nigh when the tika of our soil will anoint our foreheads." This was the cry that arrived in Kalimpong along with the calendar that had been published by the party in the new year. There was more blessed news: "They say a huge meeting will be organised in Darjeeling. People must come out to the streets now."

It was NB-sir, the Kalimpong district representative of the Party, who brought that information. "The days of fear are over," he would bluster in the villages. "It is I who brought the green flag to Kalimpong. Now our people will get justice for sure."

NB-sir would always have a green bandana wrapped around his head. A dozen boys would always mill about him. If he had to go out to the town, he would first have someone find out about the movement of the police there. Thereafter, he would swagger and boast, "I am ready to die for the soil."

NB-sir went to Chandra Singh's house with the news. He talked a bit about ethnicity, a bit about the soil, and then he said, "You are a soldier, I am a soldier. We have fought enough for the country. Now the time has come to fight for our land."

Chandra Singh understood what NB-sir had said and they left for Darjeeling the very next day. A dozen boys followed them there, even though they barely understood why they were going to Darjeeling.

Latshering was close to Chandra Singh. Not only was he Chandra Singh's right-hand man, he was also the right half of his brain. His suggestions would always form a small part of whichever course of action Chandra Singh was to take.

Latshering knew much of Darjeeling's history. When they stopped to rest at the village of Peshok, halfway up the road to Darjeeling, Latshering began a story, "This is not Peshok but Pojok. It means forest in Lepcha language. And that down there is not the Teesta, but the Thee Satha. Do you know the meaning of Darjeeling?"

Silence pervaded for a moment. No one spoke a word.

He continued, "This is the abode of God. Darjyolyang means a place where the gods smile. And Kharsang means white orchid. And Kalimpong is Kalenpong, a place where the Lepchas used to gather in the days of yore. These are the real meanings of the names of places."

Everyone was quiet. The blue Teesta flowed serenely in the valley below them.

"Ghising is a soldier. I, too, am a soldier," Chandra Singh said, breaking the silence. "We should see eye to eye. Isn't that so, Latshering?"

Latshering was dumbstruck at his forwardness. All their other associates were also surprised.

Chandra Singh then added a popular military line to what he had said: "Hindustan belongs to those who are courageous. In this country, if you want a gun, you have to ask for a cannon. If you want a pistol, you to have ask for a rifle. This is how things work here! Get it, boys?"

Their heads bobbed up and down. This meant that they had understood.

NB-sir was close to Ghising. He was not about to appear any lesser than the others. He came up with another rhetoric for his love for the soil:

"I may give up my life, I may give up my soul. But Gorkhaland, I will have anyhow."

The boys were exhausted. They kept walking silently and reached Darjeeling late in the night. Only when they arrived did they understand that what they had heard in Kalimpong was only the tip of the iceberg. In Darjeeling, even those living in the heart of town were afraid of venturing out onto the streets.

The party office was in the middle of the bazaar. But no one had the courage to sit in the office. CPI(M) goons would come to the office once a day, carrying pistols and threatening whoever happened to be present.

Latshering's voiced quavered when they entered the party office, "What a day to come here, no?"

Chandra Singh's eyes widened. Latshering couldn't speak. He turned and went towards the back of the group.

The boys were tired after walking all day and were looking for a place to sleep. Suddenly, a new rumour arrived in the office. "The CPI(M) boys are coming."

Darkness spread over everyone's faces. The boys shuddered. Latshering turned towards the door. He scrunched up his face in such anguish that it became painful to look at. NB-sir, who had boasted of giving up his life, was trying to mingle among the boys for safety when the boys, who were local residents, began to disappear one by one. In just five minutes, a deep crisis befell the office. The crowd thinned. Just then, a mob of young men arrived. They started to show off. A shorty who was wearing a red bandana kicked a chair over and shouted, "We heard that some goondas from Kalimpong have come. Who wants to disturb the peace of Darjeeling? Tell me!"

"Bloody fool, I have come! What will you do?" Chandra Singh said, standing up abruptly. He put his left foot forward, held his fists in a boxer's stance and challenged, "What wrong have the people of Kalimpong done to you? You tell me!"

"You dare talk back!" The shorty put a pistol to Chandra Singh's forehead. The boys all froze in fear. Someone leapt out of the window. A big thud, like that of a heavy sack falling to the ground, came from outside. That sound had been made by NB-sir's heavy body.

"Bastards!" Chandra Singh yelled.

The boys only heard sounds.

His eyes were shut. His fists were flailing. Powerful blows propelled by rage rearranged the faces of two boys. He then caught hold of the one with the pistol. It took him an instant to snatch away the weapon. The attackers ran off to wherever they had come from.

Chandra Singh roared again, "You will die, you sons of pigs!"

It was only then that the boys who remained in the room regained their senses. Some of them had been hiding under the table. They came out, shuddering. Others peered inside through the window. NB-sir too reappeared.

Chandra Singh was still trembling with rage. All the boys came up to stand behind him. Latshering had been hiding behind the door. He too came out slowly and stood quietly beside Chandra Singh.

What else could have happened now?

The news of the attack spread faster than the wind. "Do you know, the boys from the CPI(M), the party in power? Their pistol was snatched from them and they were roundly beaten up." Everywhere, people repeated among themselves: "The days of fear are over."

The very next day Chandra Singh became Ghising's right-hand man and started to accompany him everywhere like a bodyguard. And so Chandra Singh didn't go back to Kalimpong.

The boys who had gone to Darjeeling with him were returning home. A crowd of young people had gathered on the promenade at Chowrasta. A fat man with slits for eyes was saying to them, "The strength of a man doesn't lie in his brawn but in the power of his thinking. A man with both brawn and the power of thought— Chandra Singh is not. He is definitely not. In reality, Chandra Singh Subba is his brother, whose documents this fellow had used to join the army. This fellow's name is something else, they say. Get my drift, boys?"

Six months after this, the same man who was being spoken of at Chowrasta with another name returned to Kalimpong as the chief of the GVC.

Everyone's face had lit up. Only one face had darkened. That face was that of NB-sir, who was willing to sacrifice everything for the land.

GUNS

"THE syarpis have emptied the houses of everything."
"They have taken away the rice we had stored."
"No one has slept all night."
"No one has any grain left, even for a square meal."

These rumours reached the camp early in the morning. Nasim was surprised. Why did the CRPF confiscate the rice?

Norden might have the answer. Nasim went in search of him. One could never find Norden when he was most needed. That bastard had disappeared today as well.

It was an overcast day. The sun that was about to rise had yet to reach the camp when Chief arrived.

Nasim became alert. Surya started his report. He said, "Somebody looted the FCI godown last night. So the syarpis are raiding all houses. They have looted all the rice."

"Bastard! It was NB's boys," Chief cried. "Distribute all the rice we have in the camp among the villagers. The raids will start here in our area too! You all go to Paari, across the Relli river."

Across the Relli?

"Are you a coward? Is it easy to demand one's homeland?" Chief was unstoppable. "Now we will either kill or be killed."

He paused for a second and said, "Now the boys are coming out from their homes to join us. The sirs who will train these boys are already there in the camp, on the far side of the Relli. We must make the guns now. You all should help, got it?"

"Who will be with you, Chief?" Surya's voice emerged with

great difficulty.

"I will be with the boys from the bazaar."

"They don't have a good record. We have been receiving complaints."

"That's what happens in a revolution. We need people like them too. If the syarpis fire their guns, who will be the ones to face them? Tell me! These hooligans will be on the frontline. Got it?"

Chief smiled thinly and set off towards the camp.

The boys prepared to leave Dungra village. Norden arrived just then and heard about the shifting of the camp. He couldn't stop the mudslide of dejection that fell upon his face. It kept flowing.

Composing himself, he said, "Is it okay if I don't go?"

"Why won't you go? The syarpis are swarming all over. Didn't you hear?" Surya repeated Chief's dialogue: "If you want to die, stay here. Now we will either kill or be killed. We will make guns. Got it?"

A pall fell over Norden's face again.

Norden looked at Nasim and said, "Wait for me for half an hour."

"Why? What happened?" Nasim eyes became pitiful.

Norden went away.

He returned after disappearing for one full hour. His face was doleful. The rest of the boys had already left the room. Only Nasim was inside. Norden couldn't control himself. He started to cry loudly.

"What happened to you?" Nasim had a very kind and sensitive heart. He could never stand to see anyone weep. When he did, his own tears would fall of their own accord. The same was happening now.

Norden wept full-throated for some time. He then quietened down and, sobbing quietly, said, "I have fallen in love, my friend. With Rippandi from Bong Basti. On my mother's life, I cannot leave her!"

"What?" Nasim was astonished.

Silence pervaded the room.

Norden used to disappear sometimes. It now became clear that he used to go to Bong Basti. Nasim didn't know what to tell him. Surya entered the room, smoking a beedi. He ordered, "Let's leave, boys. It's late already."

Norden quietly took the lead. Nasim followed. And so they started a journey through the forest.

The sun had reached a point high beyond the hill. A light, cold wind had begun to buffet them. They had reached Relli. It turned out that they had to walk quite a distance uphill before they reached the camp.

The moon shone brightly in a little while. Thereafter, only the sound of footsteps could be heard. At times, the ones in front had to hack away vegetation with a khukuri to clear the path.

After they had walked a distance, they saw parts of Kalimpong on the hill across the valley, where a few lights were glowing.

It doesn't matter if the others noticed it or not, Norden's head was turned to where the lights were glowing.

Poor Norden.

*

A week passed just like that.

Across the valley, Kalimpong town would shine brightly. It would laugh along with the Himalaya in the morning and quieten in the evening. A steep footpath sloped down to reach the Relli river. That same footpath climbed up from the river to touch the camp and went beyond, to somewhere further up the hill. This was the only thing that they could see from there. Nothing else. For everywhere they turned, all they could see was jungle. There was a small school up the hill from the camp. That was where they would train. Everyone would be dressed in combat clothes. Their bodies would be covered with leaves and grasses for camouflage. Norden was wrapped up in those very same leaves and grasses. Nasim was with him. Surya had become unrecognisable. He would always have soot smeared on his face.

They would practice martial arts all day. They would run, sometimes uphill and sometimes downhill. They would hold a piece of wood and aim it as if it were a gun. They would brandish khukuris. This was how they spent their days.

Everyone would be left exhausted. Because of all the running and jumping they had to do during training, they would find it difficult to squat when they had to relieve themselves. Every time they bent their knees, they would regret it a hundred times.

Norden was squatting on the toilet. A cry went up, "Chief has arrived! Chief! Everyone, line up!"

The boys lined up on two sides of the footpath. Chief appeared in his customary get-up, surrounded by the boys. He had acquired a new swagger. Those who accompanied him had guns. Could those guns really fire? How would Nasim know?

Chief was looking stylish. A tight vest. Combat pants. Dingo boots like the one the hero of the film *Rambo* wore. He wore his hair long and sported a beard that nearly covered his face. The boys had difficulty making eye contact with him.

Nasim didn't look at Chief's face. Instead, he clicked his heels and saluted.

"Fighting is not child's play, do you understand?" Chief said, putting his hand on Nasim's shoulder. "Will you be able to stay in the camp?"

"I left everything only to fight. I forgot my home and my family." Nasim showed gumption. "I swear on Abba. I will not die before killing those who murdered Rachela."

Chief smiled. Standing beside him was a tall boy. He pulled out the khukuri tied at his hip and said, "Go, hack apart that banana trunk."

The banana tree was right next to the camp.

Nasim's legs shook. He coughed hard and said, "I am in the gun-making department, Chief."

"Your time starts now," Chief declared. "Even young boys and girls should know how to use a khukuri. Look at this Latshering!

He used to be so afraid! Now he's even better than me at it."

Chief walked up and patted Norden's back. He then turned his eyes towards the gun factory and walked up the hill.

Where did that path up the hill lead to? How could these boys, who were new to camp, know?

*

Barely ten days had elapsed. The camp became packed with new recruits.

New boys would turn up every day. In a few days, fifty boys had joined.

Surya had taken to wearing an ear-stud. Nasim was prone to dawdling; therefore, Norden would keep a watch on him.

That day, the training had started from early morning. Some boys were climbing ropes. Others were brandishing their khukuris. A dozen boys came running from the other end of the camp.

"Run to the other end and back here!" ordered the area commander chief, Naren-sir.

The boys ran like horses. The sound of their galloping filled the air. Once they reached, they turned around and ran back. A thin boy was leading. He fell.

"Who is that sissy?" Naren-sir shouted. The boy got up and ran again, dusting himself off.

The boys were still running when a new set of goods arrived in camp. A packet of phosphorous, a packet of silver pellets and ten wooden rifle butts.

It was true! The guns really would be built!

The work on the guns started only after four days. With great gusto, they all started to beat iron to forge gun barrels.

After a week or so of hard work, a dejected Nasim asked Norden, "We are about to die beating this iron. Will guns ever be made this way?"

"They say Naren-sir left the army to come here," a fresh-looking Norden said. It was clear that the memories of Rippandi had left his mind. "Just wait and see whether or not they will be made."

The three days that came after passed by in the same way, spent engrossed in hard work. On the seventh day, Commander Chief announced: "Boys, two guns are ready."

News of friends being arrested would arrive. At times, information of their own kith and kin being killed would be broadcast on Akashvani. This was the situation when the guns were being made; they became a matter of great excitement for the boys.

"Okay, now that they have been made, will they work?" Nasim doubted the iron he himself had beaten.

Commander Chief was right there. Nasim asked him hesitantly, "They will work, won't they, Sir?"

"You bastard! Don't try to be smart," Commander Chief exploded. "Yesterday's eggs, today's chickens, what do you know? You probably weren't even born when I first started to use guns. Have you heard of the battle of Burma? The story of the war with China? Those are the battles we have returned from, to fight for our own land. For the sake of your futures!"

As soon as he heard Commander Chief say that they were fighting for their own land, Surya chimed in, "I will fire the gun, Naren-sir. What do these boys know?"

"Let Chief come first," Commander Chief said. He was just an area commander. His authority was limited to the village where the camp had been set up. But Chief was the supremo of the whole of the GVC. He had to be consulted.

That very day, Chief arrived at the Lolay camp for the second time.

Commander Chief Naren-sir showed the guns to Chief. Chief looked at them carefully. He put one on his shoulder, closed his right eye and aimed down the barrel with his left eye. He was trying to say something when Surya cried, "Chief, I will try it first."

Chief turned towards Surya. He looked hard at his face and

handed him the gun.

Surya closed one eye. Norden turned away and smiled. Naren-sir showed him the target.

Surya pulled the trigger.

BANG!

"Aiyya . . . I'm dead!" Surya collapsed in a heap. Naren-sir almost lost his senses. All the boys gathered around.

"It seems bullets travel both ways down the barrel, no?" Norden asked, scared.

"I can't hear from one ear. I am dying!" Surya said, getting up slowly and wiping his face.

"What is this, Commander?" Chief asked loudly. "Is this the weapon we will fight the syarpis with?"

"This shouldn't have happened." It was as if Naren-sir's voice wouldn't emerge from his throat. "Strange! How did the bullet backfire?"

And then? They beat iron to make barrels again.

Later, the members of the Gorkha National Women Organisation (GNWO) came to the camp after collecting the "Fistful of Rice" donations. The evening sun had already disappeared behind the far hills, but the boys still hadn't finished beating iron.

Rifles

DARJEELING is a place where one can gaze at the Himalaya and bask in its coolness when the sun is scorching. If one is thirsty, one can quench one's thirst simply by watching the Teesta river flow. If rage seethes inside a person, one can calm oneself by looking at the blooming flowers.

The peaceful Darjeeling was about to burn. Could any problem be greater than this?

The days had turned monotonous. On waking up in the morning, one would feel, "Let evening fall this very moment." In the evening one would feel, "Let the morning come right now." People were neither secure in the dark of the night nor were they made happy by the bright light of day. Everyone was despondent. Worry was etched onto everyone's faces.

Yes, people had stopped smiling. There was terror, not smiles on their faces. Instead of dreams, there was fear in their eyes. Their hopeful, colourful thoughts had begun to turn ugly. Darjeeling had become different.

Amid this gloom, a piece of news spread in the camp: "They say Latshering has connections with the CPI(M)!"

"What?" This was unthinkable! The entire camp was shocked.

When Nasim and Norden returned from watch-duty, they found that that everyone in the camp had surrounded Latshering. Surya blustered, "This one had connections with the others. I found out the day before yesterday."

"Latshering, tell us truthfully! What were you discussing with that CPI(M)-wallah?" the area commander roared like a tiger.

"I didn't meet him because he is CPI(M)," Latshering said, drawing a long breath. "I met him because he is my friend. He is also from my community. That was the only reason I met him."

"What did you talk to him about?" Surya kicked at a wall in rage. That was what he would do whenever he was angry. He would kick at a tree or at a wall.

Could Latshering utter a word? The room fell silent.

"You are our old friend," said the area commander, calming himself down. "Just tell us what you talked about. Nothing will happen to you."

"It was about nomenclature. We all want a separate state. Where's the harm in asking for a separate state called Darjeeling? After all, the name of every place in Darjeeling comes from the Lepcha language. The history of this place too is linked with the Lepchas." Latshering was trembling. "The Tibetans came and destroyed the written stories of the Lepchas. The Bhutanese came and killed the Lepcha king. The British came and wiped out our language. How many times do we Lepchas have to die? This is all we talked about. Kill me if you want. I have nothing to hide."

The area commander got up from the floor and turned to Surya. He said, "Chief has asked us to release him without doing anything."

"The NB gang might finish him off if they find him," Surya said, calming down. The good thing about Surya was that he would cool down as quickly as he would flare up.

Why would the NB gang finish him off?

Lo! Those waging the revolution had already split into two factions. That day, Nasim realised something he had never thought about. He shivered.

The fight with an enemy will come to an end—you will either win or lose. But can a war against your own people ever end? You neither win nor lose.

*

The state's forces doubled three days after Latshering left the camp. The bandh was extended. Shots were fired in Darjeeling again.

The number of CRPF personnel in Kalimpong increased considerably. Jackboots would pound in the bazaar day and night. The revolutionaries would patrol the neighbourhood and the villages.

Those guarding the camp started to use code words that were changed daily.

Norden left the camp just as night fell. Chief had called for a meeting at midnight near the graveyard up on a hill. There was a big bamboo grove there, which was why that day's password was "bamboo grove".

Norden was walking alone. Wherever the person on duty would accost him, he would say "bamboo grove" and walk on silently.

The moon was gleaming brightly. One could make out travellers from afar. The only one walking quietly alongside Norden was his shadow. That too would disappear in the darkness.

It was only after he had been accosted and had repeated "bamboo grove" five times that he reached the meeting place. Chief had already arrived. A dozen boys were sitting on the ground around him, ignoring the falling dew.

A tall man began the discussion, "We must do something now. The trees we are cutting down and laying in the syarpis' paths aren't holding them back. They are gradually entering the villages. It is said that they have orders from above to shoot us."

A smaller boy who was sitting nearby got up and said, "Our fight is against the syarpis. We should snatch away their rifles and fight them with their own weapons."

Is it an easy matter to steal goats from an abattoir? Still, there was no other way. Chief got up and asked, "Tell me, who will capture a syarpi's rifle tomorrow?"

Norden thought for a moment and said, "I'll go. Give me some boys."

It was settled.

This new journey started from that very bamboo grove. Norden led the team. There were quite a few boys from the bazaar in the group. Norden would talk now and then with Kamal and Nasim. Kamal was from a different group, yet today he had been compelled to cooperate with Norden. Surya had been assigned duties in the camp, so he was left behind.

They reached Rausey just as a faint dawn was breaking. Norden wanted to go to Bong Basti. But what could he do? They had to snatch some rifles for Chief. Therefore, he caught a nap along with the others. It was mid-morning when they woke up.

They got up and marched on.

"The syarpis are patrolling Haat Bazaar." Eyewitnesses on their way back from the bazaar delivered this happy news to them.

There wouldn't be a better opportunity. They headed straight to Haat Bazaar. Three syarpis were buying vegetables. The boys quickly surrounded them.

A tall syarpi was eating a slice of watermelon. Norden pointed him out and signalled to the others.

Nasim recalled Rachela's face as she died in his lap. He sprinted, caught hold of the rifle butt and gave it a mighty tug. But the man had threaded the damn rifle strap through his epaulette. It would not spring free.

The tall syarpi was startled. He dropped the watermelon he was eating. Shouting nervously, he clutched the collar of Nasim's jacket.

Nasim quickly shrugged off his jacket and escaped.

There were many syarpi personnel milling about. They ran to save their colleague.

Kamal, who was standing at the other end of the group, unsheathed his khukuri and struck the tall syarpi in his neck. Another syarpi shoved the tall one. That made him duck. The knife missed his neck and struck his forehead instead.

A river of blood started to flow.

The syarpis started to scream in terror. The boys ran off in all directions and gathered in Rausey after two hours.

Norden had just one regret in his eyes. "Damn, I couldn't snatch away that rifle."

That regret did not allow him to sleep.

That night, the boys swore on their mothers' lives: "We will rather die than loot the syarpis' weapons."

*

The next day.

The boys had killed a pheasant and were roasting it. It was not yet midday but the raksi had come.

The kettle was being passed around in the usual way in the camp. Two kettles had already been downed when Norden asked, "Who will go with me to loot rifles?"

Nasim put his mouth to the kettle spout. He closed his eyes for a couple of minutes and declared, "I can give my life for you. I will go even if no one else does."

"What nonsense! We all have to go." Kamal quickly strapped the khukuri to his waist. "Suresh and Rabin, you stay here. Look for more raksi. After all, you bastards can't even run!"

"Let's go to 11th Mile today. They're saying only a few syarpis are there." For once, Nasim had said something intelligent.

The sun was shining hot and bright. The drink muddled their vision. A new journey had begun.

There were fewer syarpis at 11th Mile. Only three of them were patrolling the area. They had stopped at a paan kiosk and, having ordered paan, were standing there and laughing.

A syarpi with a paunch was at the head of the group. He turned towards the shopkeeper, smiled, and asked him to add extra catechu. He had a rifle. Its barrel was pointed at the sky and its butt was resting on the ground.

Would a better opportunity ever present itself?

Norden signalled to the boys. They surrounded the personnel.

The syarpi with the paunch was just about to put the paan in his mouth when Norden sprang. He caught hold of the barrel and pulled with all his might.

Baaf re! The panicked CRPF soldier bleated like a goat.

The paan fell out of his mouth and the barrel slipped from his hands. Covering his ears with his palms, he screamed and sat heavily on the ground.

Carrying the rifle, Norden shot down the hill. The boys started running after him.

After one and a half hours, the boys gathered in the village of Pudung. An entertainment programme had already started there. People garlanded Norden. He was, after all, the first revolutionary who had snatched a rifle from a syarpi.

But they had to get to camp quickly. They had to hand the rifle over to Chief. The boys left the garlands behind and loped off downhill to the camp.

This was when Nasim arrived.

"There was a syarpi camp on the other side of the bend in the road," Nasim said, drawing a long breath with a hand on his chest. "Thank god we're alive!"

Half the day had gone by. The effect of the alcohol had worn off. Baring his teeth, Norden said to himself, "I hadn't thought about that at all!"

News travels faster than air. The news of Norden's triumph had reached the camp well before he did. Preparations to welcome them had already begun.

The group finally reached the camp when night fell.

Chief was not in the camp. The area commander garlanded Norden and said, patting him on the back, "Now comes the real fight."

Surya had been staring at the goings-on for some time now. His eyes met Norden's. He smiled and said, "I will fire the rifle first. Your Surya-da won't return until he finds a syarpi. Got it?"

The Launcher

"The communists talk the talk but don't walk the walk. All their party does is produce lazy people. Now we have to shut down the factory that produces such lazy people." Chief looked away, spat, and closed his eyes.

A few fragments of chewing tobacco and spit wafted towards Norden's face. He wiped his forehead with a sleeve and looked at Chief again.

Chief issued a new order: "These communists are becoming bold again. Leave for Munsong with the boys immediately, Norden. Teach them a lesson and come back to Rausey directly. The boys should stay in the old camp now. Okay?"

The communists were still active in the tea gardens, where the plains met the mountains. A few houses in Gorubathan had been set on fire. There was no letup in the destruction in Darjeeling. It now seemed that the fight was between the red communists and the green GORAMUMO!

All of a sudden, the movement had been tagged as anti-national. Therefore, there was a realigning of objectives. Or so it seemed. The fight now was against fifty companies of the CRPF. As the CRPF's dominance increased, shots were fired in a communist stronghold of the tea gardens. People were killed again.

It had been a long time since Raju-sir had disappeared. We realised later that he had gone to Gorubathan to teach the communists a lesson. As soon he returned to the camp, he made a new declaration, "It is the members of the CPI(M) who are feeding information to the syarpis. I don't think these people who go around wearing earrings are syarpis. I think they are communists. We must do something about these guys who are troubling our people. Got it boys?"

Following Chief's orders, Norden went to Munsong at midnight, carrying the rifle he had looted from the syarpi.

What an aura Norden carried!

Baaf re! His arrival at Munsong created a furore. The CPI(M) boys went off one after another to join the Rausey camp. They all became dear to Chief.

*

A week later, Norden returned to the Rausey camp.

The camp was full.

People would come with complaints and go back with relief materials.

Just as Norden was about to enter the camp, Chief burst out in a rage. The crowd dispersed.

"You want to buy me off?" Chief's eyes were shut in anger. He pulled out a bamboo slat from the wall and shouted, "You sons of pigs! Did you bring this money to buy me off?"

A Marwari man was standing in front of Chief. His face paled with fear. He joined his hands and said, "No. We brought the money to help the revolution."

"Oi! Chase him off!" Chief yelled.

The Marwari man ran away, picking up the suitcase of money. The crowd looked on with amazement.

*

Chief began to look dejected. Only news of people being killed would arrive in the camp. The CRPF would also approach the camp on their patrols. Those on night duty couldn't even take a nap.

Chief would vanish quietly at night. He would go off alone into the jungle. No one knew where he slept. The boys were most worried about him.

Chief peered at Norden with his eyes wide open. He motioned him to come near and said, "We will meet at midnight at the graveyard in Sindebung."

Sleep disappeared from Norden's eyes. He was hungry, so he entered the kitchen. Butchers from the abbatoirs at Goskhan had brought beef. It had been a long time since he ate rice and meat.

Norden was loitering around after the meal when he saw light in Rippandi's house. He looked towards the house for a moment and drew a deep sigh.

It is in these deep, long sighs that one can find, for a little while, the things that one has lost.

That is what Norden did. He caressed Rippandi in his thoughts and went on his way.

He had to walk through the jungle. There was not much fear of the CRPF, because they too feared the night. Woe would befall anyone wearing khaki who ran into the boys at night. The boys would syack!

"Syack!" meant running a blade across their throats.

Therefore, there was more to fear from one's own comrades.

Norden was with two other boys. They reached the graveyard at midnight. Chief too arrived shortly. Raju-sir was with Chief. Surya had also been summoned. There was also the tall and thin Vijay Chhetri, Chief's new adviser.

"How can such a thin man be an adviser to Chief?" Norden had asked when he had first seen him. "Will this scrawny adviser get anything done?"

"Can our brains and the brains of the Chhetris and Bahuns ever be compared? We Limbu people are fed jaand as soon as we are born. We have more jaand in our blood than we do our mothers' milk," Chief had said, getting very worked up. "The Chettris and Bahuns are an admirable people, they don't drink liquor. Can we ever hope to match those who, for generations, haven't touched alcohol?"

Norden had remained completely quiet.

It was then that Raju-sir came to the same conclusion as Chief: "The lock which keeps a building that houses a dozen people safe is small enough to fit on one's palm. Remember, no one is big or small when all are doing the same work."

The scrawny adviser began the meeting. A cuckoo was calling nearby. Breaking the quiet of the night, Chief enquired, "Oi Bijay! The launcher is ready, isn't it?"

Launcher? The boys' excitement knew no bounds.

"Yes, Chief. I've been told it's ready. Nasim and the boys are bringing it here," the adviser said in a low voice.

"We will shoot the kakhis with it. They come down to this area every Sunday. We will frighten these bastards so that they start trembling whenever they hear the word Rausey."

"Where will we attack?" Norden asked, his voice rising.

Chief thought for some time, playing with his moustache, and said, "Tell the people of Rausey not to stay home on Sunday. We will attack near Joredhara."

The consultation was over.

Everyone returned to where they had come from.

*

Two hours later.

The police arrested two people who had attended the meeting and started interrogating them.

What if they let out the secret? Damn! The whole plan would be ruined.

Norden's forehead blazed with rage. There was a little raksi left in the kettle. He took a swig and said, turning to the adviser, "I will shoot those syarpis. Can I take that rifle with me?"

After hesitating for a while, the skinny adviser said, "A petrol bomb is ready. Do you want to take it with you?"

Aha! He had found a brick when all he had wanted was a pebble. Norden grew brave.

The petrol bomb was small enough to fit into his hand. It was wrapped in a piece of sackcloth with a wick sticking out. All he needed was to light the wick and hurl it.

The adviser taught him how to use it. The boys walked up to 11th Mile. There was a bush just above the road. The boys hid behind it. Keeping matches ready, they waited for a vehicle to arrive.

Hett! An army vehicle came first.

"Not this one. The army hasn't done anything to us. Wait for the syarpis," Norden whispered.

The vehicle went on its way.

After half an hour, another vehicle appeared. It stopped short of where they were hiding.

It was a vehicle of the FCI.

The boys ducked their heads again.

Not quite ten minutes after the vehicle had stopped, someone behind them whistled. The boys turned back in alarm.

A bearded man was standing there.

Everyone sprang up and surrounded him. Just as Norden showed the bearded man the petrol bomb in his hand, the bearded man put his hands up and said, "I am Chhabilal Sharma from the upper camp." And in a barely audible voice, he added, "Not here. We should attack in the CST area. Our friends from Kagey are also going there. In fact, they have a bigger bomb. And they're cooking rice and meat for the boys. Let's go there!"

"You're trying to trick us, you cock!" Surya had been primed to light the wick for a long time. He repeated their intention to attack from that very spot.

Was Surya ever going to listen to anyone? Chhabilal lowered his head. Then he crawled forward, out of sight.

Right then, three CRPF vehicles drew up.

The road was blocked by the goods carrier of the FCI. The CRPF convoy stopped, unable to proceed.

"Fuck! This FCI truck had to come today," Surya said with suppressed rage. He lit a matchstick.

Norden hurled the bomb at lightning speed. The whole world turned bright for a moment.

Had they hurled the petrol bomb only to light up the world?

The bomb that was meant to explode did not. CPRF personnel descended from their vehicles. Taking up positions, they opened fire.

The boys began to crawl. Chhabilal had suggested that they go towards the campus of the Central School for Tibetans. Now they heeded his advice.

The commotion went up. There was a hut a little further away. A light was burning inside the home. Someone emerged, carrying an oil lamp, but the CRPF saw a petrol bomb. They forgot the boys and ran at him, shooting.

A loud cry rang in the air. The lamp went out.

Norden, Surya and their group had reached far up the hill.

Could they return just because someone had been killed? They continued to crawl uphill. After half an hour they were near CST.

But no one was there.

"Where are the boys?" Norden asked, turning back towards Chhabilal.

Eh, surprise! There was no trace of Chhabilal. He had run off home a long time ago.

"Thoo, all that bastard wanted was company. He made us crawl so much for nothing," Surya said, dusting off his elbows. "Let me see him. I will be the first one to shoot him."

*

The next day.

The police released the boys they had arrested the night before.

They had been beaten up. But would the boys ever chicken out? They hadn't uttered a word about the night's plan.

Chief was confident.

Nasim's team reached Rausey with the launcher.

Baaf re! Where did they find this electricity pole? That was what the launcher had been made of.

"We have used nails. Marbles. Gunpowder and sand. Everything is inside this," the adviser said. The area commander was the same—Naren-sir. He grew pleased.

"We attack tonight," Chief said, twirling his mustache, "Those sons of pigs will learn that we have a launcher too."

The boys gazed at the launcher and smiled. Boys from another group arrived with jaand.

The kettle was passed around again as usual.

"I will fire, okay Nasim?" Surya once again became hot with rage.

Nasim smiled and said, "Let's reach there first."

Night was about to fall. The sun was hiding itself behind the hills. The boys set off uphill. When they reached the top, they hid themselves behind some trees and placed the launcher on an elevated spot.

"Yes. From here, we can see the police patrol when it arrives." Chief announced the plan. "The police vehicles will pass by Joredhara. We should be ready when the vehicles reach the road directly below the waterspout there. We will shoot when the first vehicle reaches that needlewood tree. We aim at the vehicle in the middle, got it?"

Surya caressed the launcher and winked at Norden.

Nasim, Norden and Surya stayed beside the launcher. Others took their respective positions.

An hour passed but not a single vehicle came.

Were they not coming today? Chief was becoming disappointed

when they saw the police vehicles on a bend in the road.

As the first vehicle reached the point directly below the dhara, Surya put the launcher on his shoulder. The vehicle had yet to reach the needlewood tree when a loud explosion was heard.

Baaf re! The unimaginable had happened. The launcher had fired this time. Smoke billowed among the trees. A vehicle had been thrown sideways towards a wall. A big hole appeared on the road.

The vehicle was full of CRPF personnel. All of them began to scream and jump out of the vehicle.

Chief shouted, "Run, boys. The job's done."

The boys ran away in all directions. The police were already panicked. When the launcher exploded, they lost their senses altogether. The khaki-clads also started to run hither and thither.

Surya ran straight downhill. His face had turned grey, perhaps because of the smoke from the launcher. Nasim was following him. They were running at full tilt when the unthinkable happened.

They came face to face with the police.

"It's over!" Nasim's eyes rolled in fear.

His legs froze. His eyes were dimmed and cloudy. Just then, sweet words resounded in lucky Surya's ears.

It turned out that the policeman standing in front of them was even more terrified than they were. Hurriedly lifting his hand, he said, "You run downhill, and we will run uphill. Try to understand, yaar."

Hett! This was the most unexpected thing that has happened in their lives. Nasim thought that he was the luckiest person on earth, and raced off towards the camp.

The khakis ran uphill.

Luckily, nothing had happened to anyone. The boys went to the jungle early in the morning to look for the launcher and brought back twisted pieces of iron. In the evening, they switched on the radio to listen to Akashvani. "Police attacked in Kalimpong. Attempt made to ambush with a launcher."

It didn't matter if any of the police had died or not. This was what they had wanted. Their dream had been fulfilled. The boys danced with joy.

Just then, Surya, who had arrived with a downcast face, said slowly, "My left ear is completely burnt. Please take a look at it, boys!"

Making Bullets Out of the Alphabet

THE scientist who dreamed of flying through the sky fell off the roof in his first attempt. Yet man never gave up on his dream of flying, which was how the aeroplane was invented.

You can say whatever you want, but history is written by those who stumble in life.

The dreams that Norden, and others like him, had dreamed were not unlike those of the men who invented the aeroplane, which was why they were being repeatedly thwarted and why they had fallen repeatedly from the roof. But it was this dream which would inspire them to get back up and dust themselves off.

"They burnt down five houses last night. They're saying the syarpis are setting fire to any houses they find unoccupied." Shocked, Surya turned towards Norden and reported this early in the morning. "Apparently, now they will shoot whoever they happen to run into. Things have become even more dangerous, boys. The police have found the printing press which prints copies of the treaty. I hear that it will be burnt down today."

The printing press which prints copies of the treaty?

Norden's eyes shut for a while. His ears turned hot. It was as if he could hear Rippandi's screams ringing in his ears. It was at that same printing press where Norden had first met Rippandi.

This happened a week before Norden and Nasim had set out to stick posters. Raju-sir had sent Norden to the printing press for the first time.

It had been announced that the Indo-Nepal Treaty of 1950 would be burnt in protest. But it had to be printed before it was burnt. Which was why Norden had gone to the printing press.

"We must burn Clause 7 of the treaty." This was the order which had come to them from the leaders higher up the organisation.

What was written in Clause 7? That wasn't his concern. He didn't even think about the matter. In reality, he was getting something printed not for it to be read, but to be burnt.

It was when Clause 7 was being printed that Rippandi and Norden entered into a treaty of the hearts.

Rippandi used to work at the printing press. She would always be punching the keys of an old typewriter. Norden would look at her. And keep staring.

"If you want to love someone eternally, love them secretly. The dream you cannot touch and the love you cannot express will never die."

This line, which he had heard somewhere a long time ago, had held him from expressing his love for a week. He wanted to love Rippandi eternally. But what to do? After a week, he couldn't hold himself back.

Love is a being with wings. One can never know when it will suddenly fly. And that was what happened. Norden's love grew wings. It rose from within his heart up to his lips. He then told Rippandi, legs trembling, "I want to marry you."

Rippandi blushed. Her fingers flew over the keys of the rickety old typewriter. To her, all the alphabets became red that day.

What more did he need?

The few letters Norden had learned finally came to good use. He cut his palm with a knife and, remembering the letters he had learned, he wrote on a page with his blood: "N+R."

On that day, Norden finally understood the power that alphabets wielded.

After writing those alphabets, he felt at peace. Very much at peace.

He carried those precious alphabets in his bag for three days; on the fourth day, he slipped it under Rippandi's typewriter.

It was many days later that the old treaty was set on fire in protest and a new treaty of the hearts was signed. And the story of Norden's and Rippandi's initials, N+R, was written.

Lo, it was that very press which was being set on fire today.

There was no difference between the press being set on fire and of their love being torched. Norden's face scrunched up in grief. Where might Rippandi be? Another fire of anxiety burned in his mind.

"It has been exactly eight months since I last met Rippandi," Norden thought, getting emotional. "I will meet her today. It may be my last meeting with her. No matter, I will see her once and only then will I die."

"We will have to salvage the press equipment," Norden said, looking up slowly at Surya. "We may not be able to go there in the daytime. But we should reach before the khakis do in the evening."

Surya didn't understand a thing, yet he nodded his head. A slight cloud had settled on his face. That was a fear of fire. Of the wrath of the flames. Of the khakis.

Days passed just like that.

The to and fro of people in the camp had not lessened. The boys readied themselves to head to Primtam Road north of town. That was where the press was.

Norden was excited. A little emotional too. He had become a little gallant but had also grown a little fearful.

Nasim, on the other hand, looked cheerful. His eyes had lit up. He had remembered his home after many days. He said, "Let's go to our house too."

The roads were being patrolled by the syarpis. The neighbourhoods were deserted. Every house they came across looked empty. It seemed as though they were not homes but merely heaps of bricks, sand and cement.

They walked through the bazaar after a long time. They first reached Norden's room. The sketches he had drawn on the wall had long vanished. Only Lord Ganesh's trunk remained, raised towards the east.

Norden looked at the house next door. An old woman was filling a vessel with water. She signalled as soon as she saw him. Norden went up to her.

"The syarpis came today as well. They were asking about you and Raju-sir." Boju glanced around and tried to shrink into a corner, "Not a single man is here. You too must run away at once. The bastards will shoot you all if they see you."

Nasim's heart started to pound. Surya's face turned pale. Norden drew a long breath and pointed towards the old road, which could be reached by taking the uphill gully.

The three walked uphill and soon reached the top. Nasim repeated Allah's name in his heart and turned around to look at his home.

Why did he have to see this?

His house wasn't there. There was only smoke from a dying fire. The house had been burnt down the previous night.

Nasim's face filled up with grey smoke. His eyes glistened with tears. Surya put his right hand on Nasim's shoulder and took a long breath.

Norden stood quietly.

When a house burns down, it does not merely mean that some pieces of wood have been set on fire, or that stones and mud have been left to smoulder. It means that an entire world has gone up in flames. Faith itself has gone up in flames. Belief has gone up in flames. Possibilities have gone up in flames. One's self has gone up in flames.

Yes, Nasim's world was burning today.

"Ughh, our house was burnt down because of me," Nasim said, kneeling. He turned to the west and said to himself, "Please protect my Abba and my Aama."

He got up slowly and said, "Let's go. We must save the printing press."

Norden was surprised. Nasim had become a different person today.

They were about to head towards the printing press when someone started to hit an electricity pole. This was a signal that the CRPF were coming. The three of them didn't know what to do. They turned in the direction of the sound and saw Raju-sir standing there.

Norden watched him in amazement. Raju-sir walked towards them. Never before had he seemed so dispirited.

Putting his hand on Norden's shoulder, he said, "Don't go to the printing press. I have sent other boys there. The CRPF have seen you."

Raju-sir kept standing for some time. He couldn't stop himself and started to wail loudly. Then, between hiccups, he said, "Our house is burning, Norden. They set it on fire. We have nothing left to call our own now."

Norden's mouth remained open. He had neither a word to utter nor a suggestion to give.

"Huh?" It was only after a long while that Norden could manage to say anything. His legs were trembling slightly. His eyes were clouded with tears.

For a while they all silently walked down the street. Then they went straight to the camp.

Half an hour after they had reached the camp, the boys brought news: "The printing press was torched today."

Norden wept for the second time that day. Those lips that had always smiled now started to tremble badly.

"We brought back a dozen typewriters. That much we could salvage," said one boy.

The boys had done at least that much, thank god. Norden felt some peace upon hearing this and wiped his eyes with the sleeve of his sweater.

"I will keep Rippandi's typewriter," he said to himself.

It was that decrepit typewriter whose keys his Rippandi would hit each day. Thank god it hadn't been consumed by the flames. That was the only good news for Norden.

He stopped his tears, tried to find the smile he had lost from his lips, and pretending to be composed, went inside the camp. He asked, "Where are the typewriters?"

"Nasim took them away," reported a short moustached boy. "They must be in Naren-sir's room."

Norden made his way there straightaway.

"I hope nothing has happened to Rippandi." He began to think about her again.

"Has every dream of Rippandi's been burnt down today?" He had turned romantic and loving after many days and, trembling, he slipped into Naren-sir's quarters.

Norden's face was flushed. He would keep rubbing his eyes and his forehead with a dirty sleeve. He took a deep breath and asked Nasim, "Give me the typewriter. It's Rippandi's. I'll keep it."

"Typewriter?" Nasim's face darkened and he said, "We've already taken it apart. To make grapeshot. Apparently, we can make grapeshot out of the typewriter keys."

Surprised, Norden said to himself, "Bullets out of alphabets?"

Silence permeated the room. Nasim didn't know what to do.

"Bring those bullets here," Naren-sir issued an order. "We must counterattack tonight."

Nasim coughed. He fished out an old bag from behind a sack. He went out, carrying a bagful of alphabets.

How could Norden know who the alphabets N+R would kill?

The Bomb

You miss those who erase every mistake you make, as if they were words written with a pencil, making space for new writing.

For Norden, Rippandi was an eraser who would rub out every mistake he made. But to be an eraser is not only to wipe out mistakes, but also to provide an opportunity to write something new.

Norden now wanted to write a new chapter, a new opportunity in his life.

For the first time, Norden forgot the thousands of mistakes he had made. He remembered Rippandi. He finally realised he had nothing but the memories of Rippandi, for which he had to live or die.

But it was true, he had no dream left in this world to chase, no path to tread upon, no land he could call his own and fall back upon. Norden, who had lost everything, had neither a dream to chase nor a path to take. He was constantly haunted by earthquakes in his dreams. Like every other resident of Darjeeling, he was constantly quaking.

"They say it is only the GVC who are fighting," Surya said, putting his hand on Norden's shoulder, who was deep in contemplation. "The rumour is that there won't be a 'land' anymore; rather, a Council will be formed. NB's boys are having the time of their lives. They have booze and girls for company. The only leader who is not hand-in-gloves with the government is our Chief."

The hills were still. Nothing stirred, other than rumours. Sometimes, a rumour would put GVC on the top of the heap. That was when Surya's chest would swell up with pride; he was one of the heroes of the GVC after all.

Today the chests were all deflated, because the rumour was horrific.

Norden drew a long breath and said, "They say there is a separate GVC faction in Labha."

Nasim closed his eyes for some time and thought.

Surya's chest became a balloon that had been pricked with a needle.

"The revolution is under our command. We are the real revolutionaries," Surya said what Chief would have said. "They are using the GVC's name to fell and sell trees. We must teach NB's boys a lesson. They are killing the poor in the name of the CPI(M) and indulging themselves using the movement for an excuse. Can you run a revolution while you keep mistresses inside the camp? Sister-fuckers . . . !"

"Mistresses inside the camp?" Norden's eyes blazed with rage.

"New GVC factions are being established," Surya repeated what he had heard, without looking up at Chief's face. "They say they have received permission from the high command to cut down trees. What should we do, Chief?"

"Now we will also attack those who cut down trees. They are already dreaming of the Council. I am a black-and-white kind of person. I cannot lie to our people. A lot of our people have died. Now, if our own leaders try anything funny, we will teach them a lesson first," Chief suddenly boomed out. "Now there will be no high command and no foot soldiers. If the revolution has to be waged, everyone must come out onto the streets. Now everyone will be equal. No one is higher or lower. Anyone who wants to be a part of the movement has to be rooted. Leaders cannot be permitted to dream of cool snow when our people are burning among hot embers. I will not let that happen. I will shoot everyone."

"Who will he shoot with his pitiful homemade pipe gun?" Nasim thought, scratching his head hesitantly. Norden and Surya stood quietly. Chief was about to say more when a voice came from behind them: "The bomb is ready, Chief."

This was astonishing. Commander chief Naren-sir had announced the unthinkable.

Bomb? The letters of the typewriters had been made into a bomb.

Naren-sir was carrying a big package. The package had been wrapped in old clothes and tied with a rope. A small fuse was poking out from it.

Chief looked at the bomb for some time. He narrowed one eye and then entered the camp saying, "Tell them the plan for tomorrow morning."

"We will now destroy the bridge!" Naren-sir exploded without preamble—it was not the bomb in his hand but the bomb of his words.

Surya went near the bomb. He touched the wick gently and said, "They say people cannot sleep anymore if they don't hear gunfire. Everyone waits for the sound of gunfire at 6:30 p.m."

Nasim laughed heartily and said, "Now they will hear a big bang! They will have sound sleep."

"Which bridge?" Norden asked, catching hold of the kettle.

The camp may run out of rice but never the firewater in the kettle. The boys would joke amongst themselves, "We must concentrate more on liquids than on solids."

"The same Teesta bridge that the syarpis use," Naren-sir started to lay out the plan. Just then, Raju-sir appeared out of nowhere. His face was still darkened by grief. The blaze which had consumed his home was still flickering in his eyes.

A middle-aged man was with Raju-sir. The man's face had been swept low with worry. His beard was greying. He was wearing shorts that were too small for him. There were no slippers on his feet.

"Take him to Chief," Raju-sir said, plonking himself down on a stone. Surya took the man to Chief's room.

Surya came back in five minutes with the grey-bearded man and said, "Raju-sir, Chief has asked us to give his pension to this man. His son has been kidnapped and he is saying that he doesn't have anything to eat at home."

Raju-sir pulled out a bag. He extracted money from it. There was a heap of loose change. He counted out three hundred rupees and gave it to the man.

The middle-aged man joined his hands in a namaste. He then headed home, basking in the sun of the happiness that had dawned on his face.

Norden's eyes were glued to the soles of that man until he had walked far into the distance; they looked like a millet field that had cracked under the scorching sun.

"Let me take a little swig too." Raju-sir asked for raksi for the first time. He brought the spout of the kettle to his mouth and said, "Surya, drink raksi. But boy, don't eat too many of those pills. You might end up offing yourself before your time."

Pills? Nasim was surprised. He now understood the secret of Surya's sudden surges of courage.

Surya turned his head away and said in a low voice, "We will detonate the bomb today. We are about to leave for the bridge."

"Bastard, not you, I will detonate the bomb today. Got it?" Raju-sir's voice had acquired swagger after two swigs from the kettle. "Sala! When a man has a house, he is always afraid that it will be destroyed. But when the house itself has been burnt down, why fear?"

Surya smiled a little. Meaning, he didn't believe what Raju-sir had said.

Just then, members of the GNWO arrived in the camp. They would come every three or four days. Travelling village to village, they would collect the "Fistful of Rice" donations and bring them to the camp.

It had been increasingly difficult to collect the donations. People didn't have anything to eat. How could they give donations again and again?

Poonam was standing at the front of the group. Her eyes met Surya's again. What should not have happened did happen anyway.

Surya became nervous. His face fell into shadow.

"Did you see the girl in the front?" Norden whispered into Nasim's ear, "That is Poonam. The girl Surya-da likes. See how red Surya-da's face has become."

Surya started to stammer all at once. Shaking, he scolded Norden, "Oi donkey, are you talking about me?" No more words came out of his mouth.

Nasim, putting his mouth to Norden's ear, whispered, "Sala, how long has Surya's affair going on, huh?"

Surya turned completely silent. Raju-sir stood up and went off inside.

The kettle was still lying on the ground. Surya finally gathered courage and whispered into Nasim's ear, "Call her bhauju and tease her. Let's see what she says."

Nasim blushed for no reason at all.

"I will tell her today that you love her," Norden terrorised Surya again. "It is not enough to love; you have to express it. I think she has come to the camp only for you."

How pitiful Surya's face became!

Surya forgot about the bomb. The CRPF. The bridge that they needed to destroy. He caressed her eyes with his and conjured up a bridge that connected his heart with hers.

Baaf re! How powerful love is. Surya, who would make the world quake, was himself trembling, for he had fallen in love.

Norden understood Surya's situation. Which was why he headed towards the camp to talk to Poonam. Surya came running up. He caught hold of Norden's hand and beseeched him, "On my mother's life, let it be for today, yaar. You can tell her tomorrow when I am not around. I will take my life if she says no."

Nasim looked at Surya's face. Dew had gathered around his eyes for the first time. They seemed at peace.

"When we get Gorkhaland, even pigs will get nuniya rice to eat. Every house will have a swimming pool." The fire-water had gone to Raju-sir's head. He walked out of the camp and started to pontificate, turning to the women from the GNWO. The women gathered around him to watch the show.

Surya put the bomb in his bag and walked off as he tried to catch a glimpse of Poonam. Nasim, Norden, and three other boys ran after him.

Only after walking downhill for ten minutes did Surya gain his composure. He turned back to face the hill for a second and said, "It's true, Norden, what you said is true. You spoke of what was in my heart. I too feel that she came to the camp just for me."

"Right! And you realised this only after coming so far? Damn coward!" At this, Surya playfully pinched Norden's cheek. Raju-sir came at a run and said, "Chief has said that we should also destroy NB's camp in Munsong tonight."

"The Munsong camp?"

Nasim stared uncomprehendingly.

"They called for such a big meeting in the Homes area. Did they invite Chief? Sala! We are ones to fight and they are ones who enjoy being close to the senior leaders." The triple-distilled raksi had really gripped Raju-sir in its clutches. He added in a rage, "It's the doing of those from NB's faction. He's always with women. We must destroy their camp today."

"Yes it's true. That's what everyone in the bazaar is saying. It is the GVC alone which is carrying on the revolution." Surya repeated what he had heard in the bazaar in the daytime. "They say all the top leaders have run off to Sikkim."

"Let's destroy the bridge first. And then the syarpis will stop moving in. After that we will raze the camp," Norden declared, getting worked up. "They are undermining our chief because he is a simple man. But we are not dead yet!"

The sun, on its way to setting, was high above the hills. The shortcut wound its way down to the main road. There was no one on the road except the seven who were heading down to the river with the bomb.

"We should explode the bomb at 6:30 p. m.," Nasim said, looking at the sun perched atop the hills. "Seems like it is only 5.30 p. m. now."

They found another shortcut from the main road. They reached the base of the bridge after walking down the shortcut for ten minutes. Baaf re! The pillar of the bridge was huge! It hadn't looked as big from the road above.

Nevertheless, their bomb wasn't small either. Norden dug a small hole and placed the bomb inside it. He then built a circle of stones around it and covered it all with sand, leaving only the fuse sticking out.

The sun had slid down behind the hills. One could hear nothing except the sound of the Teesta flowing.

"The syarpis will get what's coming once this bridge is destroyed," Surya said, looking up at the sun which had already disappeared. "Let's light it now."

"I can't do it," Raju-sir said, turning back. The potent mix of raksi and the heat of the afternoon sun had emboldened him. Now the cold had snatched away his war-like ardour. Would he ever explode the bomb now that he had sobered up?

"Surya, keep a little distance when you light the fuse." With this suggestion Raju-sir quietly slunk off.

Norden looked across the river. Three CRPF vehicles emerged around the bend. His face lit up.

"Surya, light it up!" Norden shouted. "Sala, we'll bring down the bridge along with the syarpis."

Surya struck a match. He lit the fuse and ran off into the jungle. BOOM!

The sound came after thirty seconds. And it was as loud as they had expected. Everyone's ears rang. Their eyes screwed shut. After three seconds, Nasim opened his eyes slowly.

Lo, an unthinkable sight unfolded before his eyes. The bridge was intact. Three vehicles approaching from the far side had stopped on the bridge. The syarpis had all jumped down from the vehicles and were shouting, their rifles in hand.

"Run, boys!" Norden hollered. His voice drowned out the sound of the river. The boys ran towards the jungle.

Raju-sir couldn't make it. He had just run past the crossroads at Chitrey when the police caught him.

A thin man. Unshaved. Unkempt hair. Clothes that were about to come apart at the seams. Breaths so laboured, it seemed as if they would leave his body at any moment. Raju-sir fell wholly into the hands of the police.

"I came walking from Kalimpong. I am a teacher in Sikkim," said Raju-sir. It was only his legs which weren't working, his brain was fine. He wove together a new story and narrated it. "I came on foot. Look at these shoes. Even they are torn."

Raju-sir slumped heavily on the ground and thrust the ragged shoes towards the officer.

"Sala! How dare you show your shoes to sir?" A constable kicked him. Raju-sir brought both his hands together in supplication and started to shower praise on the officer.

The officer figured out what was going on. "Where do you teach?"

"In Jorethang bazaar."

"Achchha, there is a paan-wallah there. Tell me his name and how he looks."

Now wasn't this a most awful situation!

"He is Muslim. His beard is long. He wears goggles. Everyone calls him Firoz-chacha," Raju-sir said in one breath.

Sala! Raju-sir had deserted and was teaching in Sikkim. He would come and join the revolution only on vacations!

The officer was satisfied with the answer and let him free.

Raju-sir touched the officer's feet in gratitude and quietly headed off towards Malli town. Thereafter, he never returned to the camp.

A Kidnapping

IT doesn't matter if they prick you now and then, people who are like sewing needles are the best. At least when they work, they bring together those who have been torn asunder. The dangerous ones are those who are like scissors; whenever they come into action, they tear everything apart.

Surya was like a needle. He would keep hurting people from time to time but would always keep together that which had been ripped apart. That was why the boys would always follow and support him. He now had to get together with Poonam, for which Norden was to be the thread.

It was a Thursday.

The sun was not out yet, but sleep had deserted Surya.

An earthquake was heaving inside in his heart. After all, today was the day when he would profess his love to Poonam.

For the first time in his life, he looked closely at himself.

His trousers were worn out. There were gaping holes in his shoes. His toes could be seen. He hadn't had time to shave. How long had his beard grown? He didn't have a mirror to check it. For months, the same old sweater had remained stuck to his body.

So what? Today, a rush of new energy surged through Surya. He wanted to wash his sweater. A desire to change his trousers arose in him. He wanted to shave his beard. Apply cream on his face. But what to do? He had neither spare shoes nor a clean sweater; neither face cream nor a razorblade.

There was a little water in the dhara to wash his face. He put water in his hair, tried to smoothen it to no avail and smiled, looking far off into the distance.

Wah! At that moment his face looked just like a flower that has blossomed over thorns. Like a slice of the moon hidden behind clouds.

His breath was coming short and fast, exactly like that of someone who has fallen in love for the first time. At least once in his lifetime, the one who has fallen in love performs the yogic exercise of Kapalbhati, in which one inhales through the mouth and exhales through the nose.

Surya was doing just that today.

"Let Poonam love me just once, and I will give up jaand, I will give up raksi, I will give up pills." He took a deep breath. With this fresh resolve, he exited the camp.

The camp was the same. The earth upon which he was standing was the same. The sun that had risen in the sky was also the same. In fact, everything was the same. The only thing that was new was the tiny dream that had flashed in his eyes. That was why he saw everything in a new light.

But where was Norden? He was nowhere to be seen.

The first person his eyes sought was Norden. The first name his mind thought of was Norden's, but it was that very same person whom he could not find.

Nasim had entered the camp, gasping. He took a deep breath, composed himself, and said, "There's no news of Norden's whereabouts. What shall we do now?"

He was picked up from lookout duty last night. He had been kidnapped.

The news created an uproar in the camp. The ground upon which they were standing shook. Darkness eclipsed Surya's face.

"Who kidnapped him? NB's gang?"

Surya's breath quickened. His brain boiled. He ran into his room. Picking up his khukuri, he yelled, "Motherfuckers! I will cut them down like radishes."

Nasim was standing there quietly. He knew that Norden wouldn't remain alive. It was only a week ago that Norden had buried one of NB's boys at the bottom of a terraced field.

He recollected Norden threatening NB. He recollected the day they captured the Lolay camp. And he recollected the last attack they had made on the camp in Munsong.

Chief would always say, "NB is a timber thief. The revolution is just an excuse. He burns down the houses of our own people. He burns down governmental property. Is that how a revolution should be waged? Okay, let's say Gorkhaland is created. Will Jyoti Basu[11] take away the Panchayat office? Will he break down the BDO's office and cart it off? Then why destroy them? Why burn them down?"

It was during the attack on the Munsong camp that they had captured two boys from the GVC faction there. One of them was NB's elder brother. And the one doing the capturing was Norden himself.

One of the boys they had nabbed was tall. He reeked of raksi. Every word that left his mouth was an invective directed at someone. Surya had run a blade across his arm. Nasim had covered his head with a sack and only then did the public beating start.

It was Chief's order: "Don't spare NB's toadies. They are the ones who fell trees, extort, and murder people, labelling them CPI(M)."

There was no count of how many CPI(M) cadres Surya had killed. A man whose hands used to tremble upon seeing a snake, Surya's first killing was that of a member of the CPI(M). Then he assaulted CRPF personnel. Thereafter, he knifed NB's boys who themselves were killers of CPI(M) cadres.

It was only the excuse that was constantly evolving, the work was what it had always been. To wage a revolution means to kill

---

[11] The Chief Minister of West Bengal, the state which the revolutionaries were fighting against at the time.

people. This was all Surya understood. As far as he was concerned, he had killed no one. His wielding of the khukuri was simply his contribution to the revolution.

He had cleared whichever obstacles he encountered in the path he had taken. He used his khukuri the way he was ordered to. Waged by thousands of Suryas, this was what a revolution was like.

The Suryas never asked, "Why should we use our khukuris?"

Therefore, Surya didn't ask on that day too. He set off at a run over field and fallow, brandishing an unsheathed khukuri.

But it was true, there were very few chances to consult with Chief nowadays. He would always be in a dark mood. And who else but that NB would put him in such a state? This was the extent of what Surya and Norden understood.

Nasim knew that everything had been good in the beginning but NB had overtaken Chief later on. He had set up his own faction of the GVC. Even more, he had travelled from place to place, setting up branches of his faction. It was around that time that Ghising had come for the meeting organised in the Homes area. Everyone had been called to the meeting, but Chief had not been informed. Thereafter, the genuine GVC and GORAMUMO parted ways. What was the real reason behind the split? That was something only NB's boys knew.

Norden was the one who, on that day, had thoroughly beaten up NB's elder brother. He had even injured a few of them.

That was what NB's boys wanted to avenge. They had taken Norden from the camp itself, which was even scarier. The boys of the GVC were in terrible peril. Nasim started to tremble.

"Nasim-bhai, they're saying Norden had been taken to Bong Basti." Naren-sir arrived with new information.

The boy who had come with him was quiet. He looked despondent.

"Let's go, boys," Surya's face lit up. He put his feet into torn dingo boots. Then he turned to Nasim, his face distorted with rage.

Nasim gestured to the other boys. They all strapped on their khukuris and left.

"Let's hurry," Surya said, clenching his teeth. "I will eat their flesh today."

It was not yet 8 a.m. when they reached lower Bong Basti. Naren-sir pointed, "They have kept him in that house!"

The house had a straw roof. One side was dilapidated. There were banana trees below the house and a small empty field in front. Water had been piped to the house via bamboo channels. It leaked from every joint where the channels joined each other.

The boys fanned out to surround the house. Nasim took the lead and Surya stayed in the rear. The khukuri he was carrying was exceedingly long.

When Nasim reached near the empty lot, he saw a dozen people standing at the edge of the front yard. The man sitting in the middle was Norden!

"He is fine," Nasim signalled. Surya's face brightened up. He was trying to advance when Nasim stopped him and said in a loud voice, "The house is surrounded. Free our man, or none of you will live!"

Silence pervaded the house. Those surrounding Norden looked up. No one was able to say anything. All of them started to tremble in fear.

Then Norden stepped forward and said, "Nothing's wrong, boys. These are our people. Rippandi's relatives."

Rippandi?

Nasim's mind jolted back to a day nine months ago. He remembered Norden who had wept when they were about to head to Lolay. Nasim gestured to the boys to lower their weapons.

Now the villagers were relieved. The boys of the GVC had gathered in the courtyard.

Nasim quietly went up to Norden. He had orders from Chief: "If it was NB's boys who kidnapped Norden, don't spare them. Let them know what happens when they touch our boys."

They weren't NB's boys. Nasim was relieved. Still, they had

picked up their man. So, he asked, half-threateningly, "Why did they kidnap you then?"

Norden smiled. "They didn't kidnap me. They asked me to come. I came here on my own."

Surya's eyes widened.

One of Rippandi's relatives, an old man, got up. Shaking, he said, "Our daughters are being ruined. This girl gave birth to a boy out of wedlock. When asked about the child's father, she told us this sir's name. From Kamal-sir we found that he was in this camp. That's why we brought him here."

"Don't talk about that thief Kamal," Surya got up suddenly and, rubbing his eyes, came forward. "Is the baby yours, Norden? What guarantee do you have?"

Norden sprang up. Turning his pale face, he looked into Surya's eyes. Trying to laugh, he said, "I love Rippandi, yaar. That baby is my own blood. I have explained everything to the people here. You don't understand the fate of a fatherless child. I will give him a good education."

In that instant, Norden remembered the day he left the village. He remembered the instant he slipped into the town.

He was studying in Class 2 at that time. It was the day the results were to be announced. His appa had arrived drunk at school.

Sir was looking at the results.

"Sir, has my son passed?" Norden's appa had asked, shivering.

Sir had smiled and said, "Oh, he has passed!"

Appa's chest had swelled up in pride. But then he thought of something. Norden was to go to Class 3, but he didn't even know how to write his own name. What will he read in Class 3? What was the use of such an education?

Yes, indeed. Norden still doesn't know how to spell his name.

His eyes blazed with anger; the raksi had reached the very top of his head. Norden's appa's eyes suddenly became dazed. His hands shivered. He shouted, "Sir, what do you teach your students? This child has reached Class 3, he still doesn't know how to write his name!"

He banged sir's table twice. He was about to kick at a chair when sir quickly got up and cried, "You will not threaten a government officer. I will file a police case against you, you got it?"

Appa ran away as soon as he heard the police being mentioned. The news of the incident had spread throughout the village before he reached home.

There was a taar, a big fallow field, near his house. He met Thulo Kanchha just as he was about to reach the taar. Thulo Kanchha smiled as soon as he saw appa. Teasing him, Thulo Kanchha said, "I heard you gave the sir a good beating. Now get ready to go to the Mama Ghar."

The Mama Ghar? The police station?

His senses left him. His hands and legs went limp. And he disappeared from the village that very night.

It was after that that Norden had to leave the school. To leave the village. To migrate to the city with Raju-sir.

*

Norden was an orphan. He would always look for love from those he considered his own. He had found his first love in Rippandi. Could he ever betray her? He declared with his head held high, "Rippandi's child is my child. He is my blood. Do you understand, boys?"

"Bastard, when did you manage this?" Nasim grinned. He then looked at Norden's face and entered the house. He turned his eyes towards a corner.

There he saw: red cheeks. Slit-like eyes. Hair tied up in a bun. Bashful face. There was his lovely Rippandi.

One could clearly see the glow of happiness spread across her face. That glow reflected the sun of love that had risen in Norden's eyes.

Nasim became emotional.

Norden craned his head to look. A sack, tied up into a hammock-like cradle, was in front of him. Norden's dreams were swinging inside that cradle.

"Sala! You are a fast one!" Nasim said, looking at Norden. "Now fulfill Surya-da's wish too. He has become useless, like a radish too late to be harvested. Hitch him up with Poonam."

Norden blushed. Taking a long sip of jaand, he looked at the sky. "You all go, I will come in the evening."

"Why in the evening?" Surya asked, "NB might send some of his boys to get you. Let three boys remain here!"

"No, I will arrange to send Rippandi to her village," Norden said, smiling. "I cannot keep visiting. I will come after getting someone to accompany her home. I will tell Poonam about Surya's feelings for her as soon as I return."

A smile finally rippled across Surya's lips. A new dream had dawned.

"If Poonam doesn't love me, so be it, I will be a father to her child come what may," Surya swore on his mother's life to himself.

And then he ran off to the camp along with the boys.

Shahid Ram Prasad

BUDHATHOKI's daughter had been swept away by the river.
A waist so thin, it seemed ready to come apart. Pigmented lips. An ashen face. Worn-out slippers. People used to call her a madwoman.

She would wear an old, faded kurta-suruwal. A green headband would always be wrapped around her head. Every Tuesday, she would cross the Relli river and come to Rausey on foot. She would be carrying a few vegetables, which she would give away at the camp. Promptly gobbling down any available leftovers, she would go back home after asking the same question to anyone she met, "When will Shahid Ram Prasad return?"

Shahid Ram Prasad. The martyr.

1984. Budathoki's daughter was fourteen when she first met Ram Prasad.

Ram Prasad had a ruddy complexion. He would always wear Bata shoes. An old muffler would always be slung from his neck. Mustard oil would be applied to his hair, parted in the middle. Ram Prasad must have been nineteen years old then. That was when their eyes met. And then their hearts. They eloped to start a new chapter of their life. The next year, in 1985, they had a chubby baby boy.

One could say that the times belonged to Ram Prasad and others like him!

They would toil all day and eat two square meals a day in peace. Their families were flourishing. There were small smiles on their faces and few dreams in their eyes. What else does one need to survive?

Something unexpected happened at the time. Talk about the revolution reached the village. He heard a public speech on a cassette. Two sentences in the speech moved him and got him thinking. He announced that he would join the revolution and left home.

The first sentence that had touched his heart was: "Even pigs will eat nuniya rice if we have Gorkhaland." The second sentence was: "Every house will have a swimming pool." Neither had he eaten nuniya rice nor had he seen a swimming pool. These, for him, were dreams. These dreams changed his path.

But dreams are dangerous.

Initially, the revolution was easy for Ram Prasad. All he had to do was fell trees in the hillside jungles and carry the timber up to the road. As time went by, the revolution became a little tougher. He had to fell trees and lay them across the roads. The aim was to put obstacles in the path of the CRPF. Thereafter, the revolution took a new turn. He first burned down the primary school in his own village. Then the Panchayat office. The library. He understood that there were dissenters in his own village. And so he set fire to the house of his neighbour, Dil Bahadur Thapa Magar.

Thus, Ram Prasad became a fighter. His dreams became even more colourful. He forgot his home. His son. After all, he was now in love with the land. He headed off into the jungles like thousands of other youths.

He would keep his face masked with a black cloth. On some afternoons he would come home briefly, but would disappear before sundown. There was the fear that the house might be raided by the CRPF if he stayed.

He was untraceable, like every other husband in the village.

It's true, Ram Prasad's village gradually became different. Fires leapt in that village where dreams once blossomed. The stench of gunpowder hung in the air.

There was a time when Ram Prasad's village was the most secure place in the world. No place on earth was warmer or more comforting than his hut. Come earthquake, rain or mudslide, the one place Ram Prasad would run to for safety was his house.

For Ram Prasad, his home was a mountain of confidence.

But times had changed. His house was completely empty now. There was no confidence within. No security. His world was burning in the revolution. The houses of thousands of villagers had become empty, not just Ram Prasad's. And the houses that were not yet empty only had children in them, or women. Those who were left behind lived less with dreams in their eyes and more with fear of the CRPF.

"The syarpis wear earrings. Big boots. They kick anyone they see. They have rifles in their hands. They kill any man they meet." This was all that Budhathoki's daughter understood. Every evening, she would tell her son this story. Full of fear, her son would burrow into the sack laid out on the floor and fall asleep, weeping.

Initially, Ram Prasad was in NB's gang. However, he hadn't left home to join any old gang, he had left to wage a revolution. And whatever he was ordered to do, he did.

There was little fear in his eyes. His heart was strong, and he would accomplish whatever he was asked. NB's boys needed a person just like him. And before he even knew it, he became NB's right-hand man. He realised this when the GVC attacked the Munsong camp.

That night, he understood that the movement was not what he had thought it to be.

Everyone was in the movement for the land. But why were everyone's paths different? How could Ram Prasad ever understand this?

For the first time, he understood that revolutionaries could attack other revolutionaries. On that day, he joined Surya's gang.

In fact, he had been arrested in the camp itself.

He had only one weakness: it was difficult for him to wake up once he fell asleep. He had been trapped because of that weakness.

Only after being kicked a dozen times did he realise that NB had run off to Kaffer. His boys had been captured and Surya had put up the GVC flag in the camp. Then Ram Prasad put his thumb-print on a list of those who had surrendered and gave himself up to the GVC. He became a full-time cadre of Surya's party.

And then?

He would be around Surya all the time. Once he started accompanying Surya, he started drinking. He gradually forgot home and stopped going to his village.

One evening, he was on duty in the camp. He patrolled the camp late into the night, carrying a pipe gun. At midnight he drank a little jaand and dozed off.

The sky was gloomy, and it looked like rain. A cold gust blew into the camp. Just then, the CRPF attacked.

There was an uproar. Ram Prasad woke up suddenly, but his eyes remained shut. His mind was working but his eyes remained adamantly glued together. However, he forced himself up. He was trying to pick up a pipe gun when he saw a black stump in front of him. He panicked. A syarpi was standing right before him. Their eyes met. A loud sound came just then. A rifle butt hit the side of his head. His eyes shut, never to open again. His ears went deaf, never to hear a sound again.

*

This happened in 1987. Ram Prasad's son had grown old enough to start laughing. Perhaps because there was no one in the house to look after him, he used to play in the dirt. Sometimes he would eat mud.

Budhathoki's daughter did not like her son eating mud when

there was nothing else to eat.

A famine slipped into the village. This place which used to grow crops as valuable as gold started to weep out of hunger.

The corn ran out, and so did the millet. Wild vegetables too. The buds of the fiddlehead fern were nipped as soon as they sprouted. The nettle stopped flowering. Fortunately, Magarni-bhauju, Dil Bahadur Magar's wife, was still in the village. She recognised wild yams. Half the villagers would sate their hunger with those. But now, even the yams were becoming increasingly difficult to find.

The whole village had collected a small quantity of ferns and nettles. Budhathoki's daughter carried those with her to the camp.

She had not yet had a chance to return when the day turned dreary. Clouds swirled. It started to rain. The Relli river grew fierce in flood. She couldn't cross it. She waited on the bank till late evening.

Her son was at home. She remembered her child. Her love for him swelled in her heart like an unfordable monsoon river. Yet she kept waiting there until late.

That day, Magarni-bhauju had gone to the jungle. She too had left behind her small son. Ram Prasad's son played with him throughout the day.

As the sun was about to set, hunger started to bother Ram Prasad's son. His stomach ached. His eyes kept running over to the direction from which his mother would return.

Night fell. His mother still didn't come back. Desperate with hunger, he wept. He was about to fall asleep hungry when Magarni-bhauju's son thought of an idea. He would roast cocoyam roots and give it to Ram Prasad's son.

He spotted a cocoyam plant in the yard and uprooted it. Pulling out the corm, he put it in the fire. The tears finally stopped.

After ten minutes, Magarni-bhauju's son took out the corm, still covered in ashes, and started to bite into it in turns. When he would eat, the child's eyes would be shut. He would wipe the snot off with his wrist. Then he would resume eating.

It hadn't been five minutes yet. The boy started to cry as if he would take the very roof off. He scratched his throat and vomited. Tears welled up in the eyes of Magarni-bhauju's son too. It finally dawned upon him. Sala! That wasn't cocoyam they had eaten but a poisonous taro.

The boy cried for two hours and fell asleep, weeping. When he woke up the next morning, he finally saw his mother.

There was nothing to eat at home. Her son had been hungry since the last evening. His eyes were brimming with tears. His cheeks were covered with dried snot. As soon as he saw his mother, the boy ran up to her and snuggled in her lap. He started to cry in a muted voice.

"What do you want to eat, son?" This was the only question a mother should have asked. But there was nothing to eat at home. So she couldn't ask even that. She got up and went off to the bamboo grove carrying a sickle.

A tender bamboo shoot was reaching for the sky. The sickle ran across its base. She picked up the shoot and carried it back home.

Once she had peeled the bamboo shoot, she boiled it and washed it using water and ash. She then placed it on the fireplace to cook. She felt her son's forehead. The starvation had brought on a fever.

It was only after he had eaten two pieces of the shoot that he lay on the bed, satiated.

"My child's hunger is sated." In time of famine, what can give a mother greater happiness than this?

She again went off to the jungle. She had run out of the chewing tobacco she kept in her waistband. She had an intense craving for it. Monsoon had not yet ended. The jungle was swarming with leeches, which was why she had carried a little salt. If a leech latched on, she would sprinkle it with the salt.

Even the salt was running out at home. It had been six months since they had last used cooking oil.

"Has Ram Prasad forgotten his home?" She thought of her

husband and shed some tears. For the first time, she found the situation difficult to bear. There was nothing at home. She didn't have her husband's support either. When was this revolution going to end?

She returned home after having dug up a few yams. The boy hadn't woken up yet. "Has the fever become worse?" She touched his forehead.

"My child has turned cold as snow!" She lost her senses.

She hadn't been home the previous day. When she wasn't home, the child would go everywhere and anywhere. Her mind told her, "Surely his spirit has left him."

She ran off to Magarni-bhauju's house and told her everything. Magarni-bhauju hurried to the child. Budathoki's daughter picked up a khurmi and set off to summon his spirit back.

Evening was about to set in. She started to call back his spirit. She would whistle in a low tone, dig up the ground with the khurmi, pick up a pebble, and tie it up in her wraparound.

It had been raining that day and the rain had just stopped. A cold wind was blowing. She was very frightened. She hadn't felt this much fear in her entire life.

"Ram Prasad, that scoundrel!" For the first time ever, she swore at her revolutionary husband. Her hands were shaking.

Suddenly, a loud wail sounded. The voice wept, screaming. And then she realised: her baby was no longer alive.

"Why did you give him bamboo shoot to eat when he had a fever?" Magarni-bhauju wailed, beating her chest.

"Shouldn't I have given him bamboo shoot to eat when he had a fever?" She tried to say this but the words failed to get past her throat. Only the tears kept flowing.

Magarni-bhauju was her friend in sorrow, whose house Ram Prasad and the others had burnt down. Ram Prasad's wife collapsed into Magarni-bhauju's lap.

One's limbs can be severed. One's eyes poked out. One's ears torn off. Even with nothing, one can live, and that too with a little bit of happiness. But may dreams never be shattered, else one becomes a walking corpse. Budhathoki's daughter had become just that.

Once she started weeping, she would weep continuously. Once she started laughing, she wouldn't stop. Whenever she would reach the camp, she would ask the same question, "When will Ram Prasad return?"

After she asked the question for three consecutive weeks, Norden mustered courage and told her that Ram Prasad had been killed by the syarpis. "Ram Prasad is now a martyr."

It was after that that Budhathoki's daughter started adding an adjective to Ram Prasad's name. She would ask, "When will martyr Ram Prasad return?"

People would laugh at her question. Her eyes would well up with tears and she would return from the camp.

*

It was a Tuesday.

It had rained all through Monday night, yet the arrival of Tuesday had not been overlooked by her. She had forgotten everything else but the two things in her mind: the name of Shahid Ram Prasad and Tuesday—the day she would visit the camp. Which was why she was headed there yet again. She had to meet Shahid Ram Prasad before she died.

However, none of these two things were acceptable to God. Neither was she able to meet Ram Prasad nor was she able to go to the camp. The Relli swept away her dreams.

As far as the world was concerned, the river swept away Budhathoki's daughter.

"Budhathoki's daughter was swept away by the river. That madwoman is dead." These two sentences kept echoing inside Norden's ears.

Just then, Chief arrived in the camp. He announced: "Don't send any money for the Fighting Fund. We must buy guns. Real guns. I will not allow anyone to trifle with the dreams of our martyrs. Understood, boys?"

Earlier that afternoon, talks between Chief and those in NB's faction had broken down. Fights had started between them as soon as that meeting in Pedong had ended.

In the beginning, when he had taken Chief along to Darjeeling, NB had been the supremo of the organisation, superior to Chief in hierarchy. NB didn't like it when Chief was put at the head of the GVC when it was formed, so he created his own faction and announced himself as chief. Then he travelled from location to location, setting up camps. Complaints would come from wherever the camps would be set up. Then the genuine GVC would arrive to capture those camps.

The fight was for power. That was what everyone began to understand. And thereafter, the two groups absolutely could not see eye to eye. Yet, a neutral group had come up with a good solution and had invited the warring factions for a discussion. One of those who had called for a meeting was an intellectual. And it was that intellectual who, in anger, had messed up.

He had asked NB, "Wasn't it your boys who toyed with the dignity of Budhathoki's daughter? They did the worst to her; then they killed her and disposed of her."

After that, Chief had boiled with rage. How could the meeting ever be successful?

Chief had stormed out of the meeting and announced: "If we are to have anything, it will be Gorkhaland or nothing at all. I'll shoot all those who sign their agreement for the Council."

"Don't send the money up to the high command. We will buy SLRs with that money," Chief repeated his orders. Norden kept listening quietly. Putting his hand on Nasim's shoulder, Chief issued an order, "Nasim, you and the others will go get the guns now. But be careful, those in NB's gang shouldn't know."

Just then, Chief's press secretary arrived, panting. He delivered sensational news, "The severed head of a reporter has been left hanging at Damber Chowk." That head was of the same reporter who had taken the photo of Chief published in a Hindi daily newspaper the previous day.

Chief exploded, "It's a trick to vilify us! Why would we kill an innocent person? This is surely NB's doing!"

"They say a severed head will be hung there every Tuesday," the secretary made another revelation. "On that poster is a list of people who will beheaded."

"Who else is on the list?" Surya asked, shuddering.

The secretary pulled out a torn piece of paper from his pocket and started to read. Norden was sad and surprised to hear the third name on the list.

Because that name was that of Ram Prasad. That is, Shahid Ram Prasad Tamang.

Neptay the Unfortunate

NB's boys had attacked again. They had struck the innocent Neptay in the neck with a khukuri.

A new discussion went up in the camp early in the morning.

"He made a mistake. He shouldn't have taken that road."

"If he had taken the road on the right, he would have run into the police. If he had been arrested, all that they would have done was to put him in jail. NB's boys stalk the road to the left. Was there any way for him to have not lost his life?"

It was Neptay who had been cut down. It was he who had been killed. But it was Surya who was grievously injured. He couldn't sleep that night. He couldn't even shut his eyes.

There are many sad people in the world. Yet when one saw Neptay, one would feel that there was no one sadder than him. The sigh that hung from his lips was more painful than the saddest songs sung in the tea gardens.

He was short in stature, just about as high as a tea bush. The dreams in his eyes were ugly, like the flowers of a tea bush. In place of a palace, there was a hut in his dreams. Save a square meal and a change of clothes, there were nothing in his dreams.

The land on which his hut stood, that land should belong to him. He could live with that small dream. He could die for it too.

Neptay was a human being who had been completely scoured out. So empty that he had nothing to lose. But if he possessed anything, it was a desire. A desire to see his own state being created before he died. That desire wasn't fulfilled, and that was all he lost.

Who was this Neptay, pray tell, who died even before he was birthed in this story?

Neptay was none other but Poonam's brother. Poonam, whom Surya was head over heels in love with. That was why Surya became upset when Neptay died. He could see tears in Poonam's eyes.

It was true, Neptay had no one in this world other than Poonam. He did not have land. Or sky. Or even enough rain to wet his feet. There was no sun which would warm his body. He was alone. Absolutely alone.

When Neptay, who grew up in penury, became an adult, his body, which had been affected by want, became shrivelled and puny.

Upon seeing his body, which had never experienced a full meal, the foreman had asked, "Oi Neptay, will you be able to work on the estate?"

It was on that day on the tea estate that he was christened for the second time. He became Neptay.

It was Poonam who had pushed him into the whirlwind of the revolution. After all, for Neptay, she served as his eyes and mind, seeing and thinking for him. The feet that walked for him. Wherever Poonam went, he would go.

The day that Neptay took his first breath in the world was the day that his mother breathed her last. Thereafter, the first step he ever took was with his hand in Poonam's. Poonam was his sister. His mother. His everything.

One day, Neptay walked into a cowshed fenced with bamboo. That was his first school. That's where he saw the alphabets for the first time. He was nearly nine years old then.

There was a sister at home. His father too. To have a father is to have everything in the world. So what if he had lost his mother? For Neptay, his father was both earth and sky.

When he would head off to school carrying coarse semolina rotis for lunch, his sister would go to the tea estate with a sickle. His father would pedal up the hill on his rickety bicycle to Chuikhim.

He would mine coal, load it up on his bicycle and cart it downhill. There he would sell the coal and the evening meal would be assured.

It was exactly six months after he began to recognise the alphabets that Neptay wrote his name. He understood a new thing that day: the person who led him by the hand was not Didi but Poonam. That skin-and-bone man who sweated day and night for him was not Bau, his father, but Budang.

That is, he learned the names of his sister and father that day.

A month later, monsoon season was advancing quickly. It was raining continuously. Bau had gone out to dig up coal. There was a holiday at school and he was playing on the porch. Suddenly, his sister arrived at a run. She threw the bag on the floor and started crying and howling.

Just as Didi was about to faint, he understood. Bau had been crushed under the earth. He was buried inside the coalmine.

Neptay kept standing silently. Tears brimmed at the edges of his eyes, but they didn't fall. His hands kept shaking for a long time.

From that day onwards, he forgot how to weep. He learned to live with the burden of life.

The next five years passed just like that. He dropped out of school. He forgot the alphabets. He started hauling and selling coal to survive. Then the revolution for the land began. He, along with Poonam, flung himself into the revolution.

Neptay had been everything to Poonam too, her little brother whom the NB faction had needlessly murdered. Neptay had become a martyr. The revolution had taken everything away from Poonam.

Surya couldn't bear to watch Poonam cry. This was why he couldn't sleep all night. Surya, pale with grief, got out of bed early. Looking woebegone, he kept staring at Norden.

"They say NB has planted an informer among us," Norden said slowly. "Our news is leaking. Neptay and the others were killed because of that informer."

For a while Surya was stunned. Then he closed his eyes, swore on his mother's life and said, "I will not spare that NB now. And let me just find out who that informer is; I will bury him alive."

Norden was about to go out, carrying rough cardboard paper. Just as he reached the door, he turned towards Surya and said, "You must have heard that Poonam has returned to the estate?"

Surya became sad. Terribly sad.

Norden hurried out. He went to Naren-sir's quarters and said, "Naren-sir, Chief has asked us to make a cartoon of Ghising. What is a cartoon?"

"You idiot, when it was time to study, all you did was run around with a catapult in hand," Naren-sir said, smiling. "Chief wants you to make a drawing of Ghising."

Norden began to draw for the first time in months.

He thought of this and that for a long time. Then he sat on the floor, fully focused. He crossed his legs. Ghising's face, which he had seen a few times, danced before his eyes. He drew Ghising's face in two hours. Ghising's cap, drawn in pencil, looked exceedingly beautiful. He looked at the drawing for a long time and headed to Chief's quarters.

There was a commotion in the room. Nasim, Surya and Naren-sir were present. As Norden entered the room, the talk veered to NB, and then to Raju-sir.

"Has the money from Alaichikhop really not come?" Surya saw red.

Chief thundered, "Hadn't I ordered all of you to not collect money of that kind?"

"No. There was no one from the Party at home. But there was a big bundle of money underneath the bed." Surya was reporting an incident that had happened three months earlier. "Kamal had stuffed all the money into a bag. When we asked, he said it was for the Fighting Fund. The money couldn't have been any less than one lakh rupees."

"Did anyone else know that Neptay was working for us?" Norden said, drawing a long breath. "That must have been Kamal's doing too. He can do anything for money. Some revolutionaries report our locations to the syarpi. Others act as NB's middlemen. Who can we trust?"

"It has been more than fifteen days since Kamal has vanished. He must surely be with NB now. We have no choice but to procure weapons," Chief thundered. "You two go get rifles. We have people in Naxalbari. Carry the money in that bag. Make sure that NB's boys don't get a whiff of your mission. You might get yourself killed, like Neptay."

"Those goons rammed a crowbar down your own brother's throat and killed him. It turns out that the information about him going to the jungle to get weapons had also been leaked," Norden said, showing the drawing he had made to Chief. "This time they will die. I will also go to fetch the weapons. Let Naren-sir watch over the boys. The three of us will go."

Chief looked at Norden's face. Then he acted like he was calming down. Thereafter he kept steadily examining the drawing.

Suddenly, his face changed. His eyes shut in anger.

"You buffoon! What is this? Is Ghising your king?" His eyes opened wide. Stamping the ground, he said, "I'd asked you to draw a cartoon!"

Cartoon?

Norden didn't get it.

"This is not a cartoon," Naren-sir explained. "The eyes should be big and stretched. The nose should be disfigured. The lips puffed up. So that people laugh at his face, you know."

Nasim looked into Norden's eyes, smiling.

"I don't know how to draw like that," Norden said, grinning. "I have even forgotten how to sketch."

"Forget about the cartoon-sartoon," Chief said, calming down. "Take that jeep and leave at 3 a.m. Be careful. We have enemies everywhere. The police on the one hand, NB's boys on the other. Don't drink on the way. Have you understood?"

"We don't need informer friends like Kamal." Surya clenched his teeth. He then calmed down and said, "We have to quickly drop by Poonam's house if we can. There is no one in the world to wipe her tears."

Norden understood. Surya wanted to wipe away Poonam's tears himself.

In a place where every dream is illegal, how justified is it for a sorrowful individual to dream of wiping away the tears of another? How could Surya ever understand that?

Norden looked into Surya's eyes for a moment.

He saw: A little anger. A little rage. A little sorrow. A little fatigue. A little love. A little betrayal and that same illicit dream.

A dream that wanted to roam free on this earth.

Norden the Lame

LIGHT had yet to fall upon the earth. Clouds were swirling in the sky. The temperature had dropped considerably. When speaking, dense vapour would emerge from the mouth before the words came.

Norden wrapped an old towel around his shoulders. Nasim picked up the bag of money. He peered quickly into the bag and took a seat in the vehicle. Just at that moment, a rooster crowed in a distant village.

Surya wrapped a black muffler around his face like a mask. He already had a khukuri slung at his waist. Three masked men followed him. They took the rear seat in the jeep.

"Uff!" A big plume of condensation escaped the driver's mouth. The jeep wouldn't start. The masked men in the back got out and pushed the jeep three times. Only then did it start moving.

Main Road, which ran through the heart of town, was silent. The police station was deep in slumber. The jeep headed straight towards the Teesta. They were about to reach 3rd Mile when they found a mound of stones blocking their way. Two of the masked men jumped out.

A dim light was falling on the ground. Two shadowy figures flickered at the bend in the road.

"Those are the thieves from the GVC," one of the shadows cried.

"Surrender immediately, understand? If not, don't return this way in the evening," another shadow shouted. "Now you won't live!"

"You corpses! I will drink your blood!" Surya jumped out of the jeep. So did Norden and Nasim. Would the two masked boys allow themselves to be left behind? They ran towards the bend, khukuris in hand. The two shadows disappeared in the darkness.

"Now we cannot take this road in the evening," Norden said, taking a deep breath.

The masked boys cleared the stones. The jeep started. They reached Teesta at dawn. The breeze coming off the river brushed past their ears. The sweat on their brows from earlier finally dried up.

Vegetation had nearly covered the cliffside walls that formed one side of the highway. Two bends on the road were about to topple into the river because of rain. The river was sleeping underneath the cover of a light mist. The jeep travelled along the lip of the highway, with the river flowing immediately below it. Climbing uphill, they were about to reach the top of the rise at Birik Dara when a middle-aged woman signalled the jeep to stop.

"Why are you stopping the vehicle?" Surya shouted at the driver. "Run her over. Let her die."

The driver slowed down further.

"Do you want to die?" Norden cried, flummoxed. "What is it with this damn driver? Is this a taxi?"

"No, she is one of our own," the driver said, pulling the towel down from his mouth. "That's Reshma-didi, the one who used to come to the camp with Poonam."

Poonam?

Surya's face brightened.

"What happened to you, didi?" asked Nasim, looking out of the window. "Where are you going?"

"The syarpis have swarmed the place, they're suspecting that the GVC boys will be travelling to buy arms." Reshma-didi inhaled a long breath. Then she exhaled a plume of mist. She continued, her voice trembling, "Don't go any further. The syarpis and the GNLF boys are keeping a watch at the next bend in the road. Everyone's saying that our revolution has reached a compromise with the government. Is that so?"

"Where should we go now?" Norden asked, his face wilting. Reshma-didi ran off over a kutcha road. The driver parked on a bend on that same road. He said, "We won't be able to return today. The boys must have gathered all over 3rd Mile by now. It doesn't look like we will survive today, boys."

Surya came up with an idea. "Let's walk along the banks of the river. We are about to reach Kalijhora. We will get to Baghpul in three or four hours."

Norden took out the khukuri from the jeep. He made Nasim carry the bag with the money. Thereafter, they climbed down to the river behind Surya.

By now, the light had become strong. The sun was out. All around, one could see nothing but the silent trees. Down below them, the Teesta was flowing, sighing sorrowfully.

"If anyone sees us, we're finished!" Nasim walked steadily, carrying this fear in his heart.

It was impossible to reach the river. In some places the water reached right up to the bank, especially on the river bends. They took a path that ran a little above the river.

They had covered quite a distance when rain came out of nowhere.

All of them took shelter in a cave. It rained for nearly three hours before relenting.

"Let's go," Surya said, looking up at the sun above the hills. "I think it's past noon."

They came out of the cave and resumed walking. Soaked in the rain, the leaves of the broom grass had become like knives. One touch and they could sever a finger.

They had walked for another twenty minutes when something exploded on the road above. All of them shrank against the broom grass. It was difficult to make out if they were breathing or not.

The movement and activities of the CRPF on the road suddenly increased. Faint sounds of people talking and moving floated over to them. In a situation like this, who would dare to move?

"Look at the river below!" Surya's quavering voice reached the others' ears. A large group of men were standing on the bank.

"These boys belong to the party. Looks like NB's gang," Norden said, killing any hope of heading forward, at least for the day.

"Let's head for that crevice," Surya said, gesturing ahead.

The masked boys were petrified. Their hands started to tremble so badly that they would have fallen into the Teesta if their grip on the broom grass loosened.

At times, life throws up such terrifying moments in which one gives up on everything. One forgets everything except one's own life.

This was precisely such a moment. Let the money go to hell. Let the weapons be bought. But their lives—they could not lose them.

And so, to save their lives, they all slipped behind another rock.

What if the syarpis swarmed down on them from the road? What if NB's boys came along the river? What if the firing started from that small outcrop?

When a man is gripped by paranoia, he may run to the other end of the world, but the fear in his heart will keep killing him.

That crevice had become the most insecure place on earth. They could neither get out of it nor hide there without worrying.

"We made a mistake by leaving the jeep, boys," Norden said, shivering. "That's what told them we are hiding somewhere. Don't even dream of going ahead."

"Damn . . . That's right!" Nasim said, looking into the driver's eyes. There was nothing except the fear of death in them. There wasn't a single glimmer of hope. To look at the driver for a long time was to panic. He did not want to look at the driver. Instead, he said in a low voice, "What options do we have? What will we do?"

The boys who were on the riverbank stayed there till evening, basking in the sun until it finally set. They returned along the river.

Could they think innovatively when they were half dead with hunger? All of them declared that they would sleep in the cave.

*

The struggles waged by man. The battles fought by man. Everything man does is ultimately for his stomach. That night was their first bitter experience in a long time. It was a night with neither sleep nor dreams. It was a night with nothing.

There is no greater enemy than fear, terror, hunger, thirst, and greed. Yes, that night was the night of the enemies.

The boys drifted off to sleep only near the break of dawn. They had just fallen asleep when a cold wind began to buffet them. Their slumber kept being interrupted. It was dawn when they woke up.

Norden slowly opened his eyes. He saw Nasim on his knees in front of him. Nasim's eyes were closed, and he was thinking of something.

"What happened?"

Nasim turned around five minutes after the question was asked and looked at Norden's face in silence.

"Fool, aren't you the one who dreamed of firing guns?" Norden tried to force laughter.

"Today is my Abba's birthday," Nasim said, taking a deep breath. "We think of our fathers only in grief. I saw Abba in a dream this morning."

"You don't need shade from the sun if your mother is with you. You don't need a shelter from the rain if your father is with you," Nasim said, recalling his pre-revolution schooldays. His face turned dark, like a day of rain. "Whatever Raju-sir said was right. I have understood that today."

Norden could not properly recollect his father's face, but he had a memory of him. His appa used to go down to Oodlabari, sometimes with chilies, at times with ginger and at others with bullock hides. He would return in the evening with puffed-rice balls sweetened with jaggery. The night of his return would be the most beautiful night of all.

One Sunday in winter, his father had walked down to Oodlabari along the Ghis river with bullock hides. He never returned. That was the last night when Norden waited all night for the puffed-rice balls. But no, his father didn't come back.

Just as he was beginning to forget his father's face, the news spread throughout the village: Norden's appa fled because his teacher had threatened him. Apparently, he had slipped into Assam to work in the coalmines.

"Yes, Raju-sir said it right," Norden said to himself. "To not have a father is to suffer."

Surya brought some wild bananas. They were half-ripe.

Norden's face brightened up. An entire comb of bananas was strewn before him.

Nasim forgot his Abba. Norden forgot the sweet puffed-rice balls. It had been nearly twenty-four hours since they had eaten anything. All of them attacked the bunch of bananas.

The entire bunch was finished in ten minutes. There was a heap of skins on one side. On the other was a pile of seeds.

The forest was eerily quiet. The dew had turned everyone's hair white.

"Let's go," Nasim said, puffing out a cloud of vapour, and shouldered the bag of money.

The Teesta was flowing silently over the riverbed below them. More dew fell. The atmosphere was oppressive and closed in on them from all sides. Their hands turned stiff with cold, and their clothes were soon soaking wet. Nasim adjusted the bag on his back and started to walk. There was a small landslide a short distance ahead.

"Walk slowly," Norden said. "Even if you fall down, make sure that the money doesn't."

"You bastard . . ." Nasim had just turned around when they heard gunfire from the road above.

If one was to make a guess about their location, the boys turned to look upwards at the village of Kalijhora.

The commotion increased. People started to shout. The sound of vehicles could be heard. The group stayed close together, pressed against the wall. The commotion lasted for nearly an hour.

It seemed that the sun would come out, but the rain started again. It was difficult to keep the money dry. There was no cave or crevice nearby. Even as they tried, currency notes worth one lakh rupees turned into a lumpy mass.

The cold bananas they had eaten in the morning hadn't been enough. Hunger was waging the epic war of the *Mahabharata* in their stomachs once more.

The uproar was dying down. Norden peered upwards. The road wasn't too far above them. Whenever the Army trucks moved, their sound would come right to their ears. Then they heard the sound of marching boots. Their collective breathing stopped, and they sat there with their heads hidden among the bushes of broom grass.

"Have you burnt down the vehicle? Lop off six inches off of them wherever you meet them." The sound of a deep voice came faintly to their ears.

The boys from the party had torched a vehicle. This was getting worse and worse.

"We should wait at the railway crossing," another voice shouted. "They couldn't have crossed over into Siliguri already. Keep watch through the night, got it?"

Baaf re! That was Kamal's voice.

Just then, they heard the sharp sound of an engine starting up. The marching boots boarded the vehicle and headed to Sevoke.

As soon as the vehicle started, they heard someone cry. It was their driver. He was standing on level ground a little further away. He squatted, rested his chin on his knees and wept, clutching his dishevelled hair.

"Why are you crying, boy? We have our lives at least," Nasim said in a low voice. "Surya-da, I don't think we can do anything now. The money is a soggy mess."

Norden had thought that Surya would explode, but nothing of that sort happened. Surya, who was always incandescent, was about to be extinguished by hunger, thirst, and fear. He was helpless.

"We shouldn't return via this path even on pain of death," Surya said, after thinking for a long time. "Let's do this instead, let's cross over to the other side on the cable ropeway at 27th Mile."

Norden had no alternative other than to nod his head. The driver wanted to see his burnt jeep one last time, but that was impossible. He kept sobbing for a very long time.

*

The sun was about to set when the return journey began. They reached 27th Mile as dusk fell. It was where the old ropeway stood alone, weeping quietly.

They spent some time there sobbing along with the song of the river. The sound of the flowing Teesta was so loud that it was difficult to hear anything on the far side of the bank. After a long while they saw someone on the far bank. Surya signalled to him. The carriage-basket used to transport goods came swaying towards them.

"Not all together," Norden said. "Nasim, you take the money and go. We should be ready here in case anyone comes."

Nasim became the sacrificial goat yet again.

"I carried the money for nothing," Nasim thought and walked off. The masked boys preceded him. Nasim, his legs made useless by nervous trembling, finally managed to climb into the carriage-basket.

Surya whistled. The carriage-basket glided over to the other side. Only then did Norden, Surya and the driver climb into the basket that had glided to them along the parallel line of the ropeway. On its second trip, the ropeway leisurely made its way to the opposite bank of the Teesta.

Will you believe this much? Now the chances of these seven comrades surviving was greater than of them dying.

*

Uff! What a dark jungle.

As soon as they crossed the river, the road uphill narrowed. Evening was falling. Darkness engulfed them due to the dense forest.

At last, they came to a stream after they had walked for some time. They had nothing to eat. Soaked in the rain, their clothes had become heavy. A strange smell assailed their noses. There was a cave behind a rock, which soon became a secure place for them.

Nasim entered the cave. He opened the bundle of money. If anyone had seen the state of the money, they would have jeered, "The guns which you would buy with this money, will they even kill anyone?"

The image of Mahatma Gandhi on the currency notes, wet and miserable, was peering morosely at Nasim. He was peeling off one note after another like one would an onion. The wet notes remained glued to each other, as though they had vowed to never get separated.

"What will we eat now?" Norden asked, looking up and scratching his head.

The masked boys had taken off their facial coverings in the afternoon. Having wrapped those same pieces of cloth around their heads, they were squatting on the ground, shivering in the cold.

"You donkeys! Go, cut that banana stem and bring it here," Surya spat. "We will eat its core. That will see us through the night."

One masked boy went lazily to the tree, cut it, extracted the core and came back to the cave.

"I shouldn't have gone to Raju-sir's house that day." Nasim had become weepy. He nearly shed tears. Then, composing himself, he said, "If we survive, maybe we should surrender ourselves to the

GNLF instead."

"You will surrender, will you, bastard?" Surya still had some spirit left. Munching on a piece of the banana core, he said, "We will die but we won't become traitors. Did so many people die just so that we could get a Council?"

"We will survive, won't we?" the second masked boy finally made himself heard. "I am still single. Will I die before I caress the girl I like?"

"Am I married, you fool?" Surya exclaimed, gesticulating. "If we were to die, Norden's son will survive. Who will we have to leave behind? This one did the right thing. You sent your wife home, didn't you?"

Norden remembered his son and wife Rippandi after many days.

"What will happen if he survives? He will probably live in grief and suffering like I did," Norden said. "Neither can I remember my appa's face nor will my son know mine. If I die, he will suffer."

Everyone became quiet.

"Appa has never come to me in my dreams," Norden thought. "If I die, perhaps I too will never reach my son's dreams."

His heart soured. He looked at Nasim. He was still busy disentangling the currency notes.

Surya was thinking, his back pressed against the wall. His eyes were shut. Norden's face turned dark like a moonless night.

The masked boys were busy munching on the banana core. The rain started to fall again.

Sleep visited no one that night. Only dreams did. Those dreams would begin and end in sorrow.

Yes, that was the most sorrowful night of the world. The darkest night.

The faint light of dawn appeared after they had tried to shut their eyes for the thousandth time. Surya came out of the cave upon seeing the light.

"Let's go!" Surya showed them a glimmer of hope. "Looks like we're somewhere near Najok. Now we won't die, boys."

And?

That day's walk began. This was the walk of the revolutionaries who were tormented by hunger and thirst, revolutionaries who had no dreams of the future in their eyes, only a great deal of sleep.

They had nothing. No path to walk on. No courage to run with. And no goal to reach either.

The weather finally cleared. The sun's rays fell on the top of the hills. They reached Najok.

There was something like an old, fenced shed nearby. In front of it was an ancient wooden house. Smoke was emanating from its roof.

"We must get something to eat even if we have to threaten these people with our khukuris," Surya said.

The masked boys donned their black masks again. Nasim was following them, Surya and Norden led. They surrounded the house and shouted, "Give us some food to eat if you have any. We are revolutionaries. We haven't eaten for three days."

An old man came out, coughing. He looked straight at Surya and said, "This is my brother's house. There is nothing to eat here. In my house, I could have given you tapioca. But you are not safe here. The GNLF people have been looking for you since last night, khukuris in hand."

Surya's mind went blank. The boys' masks nearly fell off in astonishment at having been found out.

Norden tried to bluff his way out.

"No, we are from the GNLF. We were going to hand over some money to Ghising but the syarpis didn't let us pass. So we fled and came here."

The old man's face changed.

"You needn't lie to me. I am a teacher in this village," the old man said, rubbing his eyes. "I know that you are from the GVC and the GNLF is looking for you. If you will heed me, stay here for some time. I will get some corn roasted for you."

The old man spoke to someone inside the house, "Kainla, roast some corn for these boys."

Nasim really liked what the old teacher had said. The man who gives you one square meal when you are hungry is one of your own. He felt that the teacher was someone dear to him. So Nasim came up to the man and asked him, "And which group are you from? GVC or LF?"

The roasted corn arrived. The boys took off their masks and started chewing hungrily.

The old man smiled. "Those who raise slogans in the name of land till Tuesday evening embrace Communist cadres and debate with them on Wednesday morning. I'm not sure what gets into their heads, but on Thursday they start mouthing speeches about nation-building and play with fighting-sticks at the RSS shakha. On Friday, they boil some flour for glue and, talking about secularism, stick Congress Party posters at Damber Chowk. From all this, they earn a little money with which they buy groceries at the weekly haat on Saturday. What can we expect from leaders like these?

"Only a creature that doesn't possess a stomach can be honest in politics," the old man continued. "The sacrifices you are making for the revolution—these leaders are using it for their own political gain. Do you understand what I mean?"

The old man went uphill, coughing. The corn on the plate had been finished.

The boys didn't understand what the old man had said. They headed off into the jungle again.

After they had walked through the Najok jungle for a little while, the sun's rays began filtering in through the trees. It was the first sunny day they had seen after three days. Surya's face brightened a little, but the driver's face was still downcast. The sorrow of not being able to see his destroyed vehicle was reflected on his face. Nasim was feeling confident that the drenched currency notes would dry off now.

"Oi, don't you dare run off!" someone shouted suddenly.

Lo, the unthinkable had happened. The boys had walked into a trap.

Suddenly, the jungle turned dark. Completely dark. Silence pervaded all around. It was all over for them.

The masked boys lifted their hands in surrender. Surya unhooked the khukuri at his waist and laid it down on the ground. Nasim wasn't willing to let go of the bag.

A bearded man stepped forward and asked for the bag. Nasim handed the bag worth one lakh and thirty thousand over to him. He then knelt down without saying anything.

Many boys were accompanying the bearded man. More than two dozen of them were carrying khukuris. They had also brought ropes with them. One after the other, they tied up the arms of the seven comrades and made them walk uphill.

They reached a village just before dusk. The bearded man ordered, "We have to take them to Kaffer tomorrow. Give them a little beaten rice to eat and keep them here. Guard them all night. The thieves might run away. Take off their ropes for now."

Kaffer?

A festival of blood would take place on top of the Sailunge hill in Kaffer. To go there was to die. Chief's brother had been cut to pieces in that same place. Nasim shivered.

Norden had heard the story of Chintu and Mintu. Both of them used to sing songs. Beautifully. They were members of the GVC and had been caught and taken to that hill. They were half buried in the ground and made to sing throughout the night. Come morning, their captors played soccer with their heads and killed them.

"Oi, aren't you the one who eats human flesh?" A strong boy stepped forward. He kicked Surya twice on his back and said, "What does it taste like, tell me?"

Surya got angry. "Thoo, you bloody dalals!" He spat on the boy's face.

What else could have happened next? Fists rained down on the boys. They were thrashed like bullocks tied up to stakes. Nasim received a cut on his head and blood began to flow. Surya's eyes were shut.

The masked boys looked even more pitiable. Just then, another leader arrived.

"That's enough! Untie their hands," the bearded man ordered. The attackers untied them. The comrades all collapsed on to the ground.

Norden was very thirsty. He raised his head and whimpered, "Water . . ."

"Here, water." One boy urinated on Norden's head.

"Give him water," the voice issuing the order sounded familiar. It was a kind voice too. Norden couldn't help but look. He raised his head a little and sneaked a glance.

Baaf re! He was the same old man who had gotten someone to roast corn for them to eat.

Someone brought a cup of water and gave it to Norden. Norden wanted to say something but couldn't.

They were kept in a cow shed. All around them were dried corn husks. Even if they moved a little, the husks would rustle.

Half an hour after he drank the water, Norden nudged Surya on his shoulder. Surya raised his head a little.

Norden said in a low voice, "The one who got us arrested was the one who got us the corn to eat."

The flow of blood from Nasim's head had stanched a little. He too raised his head and whimpered, "To reach Kaffer is to die, understand that."

Surya looked towards the door and said, "Act like you're dead. In the morning, we will run away."

The driver looked at them with piteous eyes and said, "It feels like my leg is broken. I cannot even run. What should I do?"

He was a moaner. He started to weep again.

The sound had reached outside. A short boy came running and hit him with a length of firewood.

Everyone stopped breathing once again.

So what if they had been soundly beaten? They had found a warm place to sleep in after three days. Their eyes didn't stay open. When Surya opened his eyes the next morning, the light from the sun was already falling on the ground. He lightly nudged Norden.

Norden opened his eyes and cursed inwardly, "Thoo, sala!"

Someone was talking close by. One of the masked boys had made friends with the enemy. A guard who had formerly been with the GVC. He was chattering merrily away.

After they had all woken up, the guard went out of the shed.

"The guard said that we needn't worry much. But they won't spare Surya, Norden, and Nasim." The masked boy let them in on a secret. "You all should run away. I will keep them busy."

"How?" Nasim asked the most serious question of his life.

The guard, the masked boy's friend, came back to the shed.

"I have spoken about the matter to the rest. You know, the fact that you will surrender," he said, winking. "Want a betel nut?"

"Yeah, sure." The masked boy got up gingerly.

"The thieves have beaten us up badly. You also delivered a few blows, didn't you?" the masked boy asked. "So, are we supposed to shit here?"

"Go over there," the guard pointed at a lantana bush outside.

The masked boy went out, limping.

"Oi, where are you running off to?" someone outside shouted. The boys gathered around immediately.

"May I please shit, sir?" The masked boy's eyes welled up.

"Look at him, boys!" the teacher who had had the corn roasted for them said, laughing. The boys on sentry duty laughed at the pitiable situation the masked boy was in.

"Jump, boys!" Surya shouted and jumped so hard that he cleared three terraced fields at once. Norden jumped with him. Nasim followed suit. The driver stumbled on the lip of a field and fell down. The boys caught him immediately. Limping, he started to cry loudly.

The other two masked boys were looking on with their mouths agape. The one who wanted to shit had already been surrounded by the boys. One group gave chase, shouting. Even as they watched, Surya, Norden and Nasim disappeared into the jungle.

The boys chasing them did not have a chance to pick up their khukuris. They kept up the chase, hurling stones at their quarry.

They kept running for a full one-and-a-half hours. Only then did they see the bank of the Relli river.

Without thinking anything Surya jumped off a tall cliff. Norden jumped too. After all, he wanted to live. Nasim also followed, closing his eyes.

Nasim couldn't get up from where he had landed. A stone had pierced his shoe and then his foot. It became bloody. He lay there, clutching his foot and crying.

Three days of continuous rain had swelled up the river and it spanned the bank. Still, one had to cross it in order to live. Surya jumped into the Relli and swam across it.

Norden looked at Surya, who had already reached the other side of the river, and then at Nasim, who was doubled over in pain.

"Run, run," Nasim gestured with his hand. Norden jumped. He swam for a while, but the current didn't let him cross and swept him down two bends in the river.

Surya made his way up the hill slowly.

Those who were giving chase watched Surya from above for a long time. They didn't dare jump down the cliff. They eventually retreated.

And?

Norden, who had been swept away by the river, finally emerged on the bank. He was limping. His left leg had become a hindrance to him. But he still had his life, so he didn't stop running. He kept running along the bank, dragging his crippled leg behind him.

It was only after he rounded a bend in the river that his leg moved out of sight, still limping.

*

Soon after Norden disappeared, carrying the injury on his leg, the revolution too lost steam. A separate state of Darjeeling wasn't formed, but the Gorkha Hill Council came into being.

The Final Story

"That was where I last saw Norden," the bearded uncle said, concluding the story around the time the rooster began crowing. "Now tell me, do you think Norden lived or died?"

He had ended the story with the same question that I had tried to find an answer for. In fact, it was the same story for which I had sacrificed sleep for a whole night.

Was this how it should be? I turned to Ripden, yawning widely.

Poinsettias were blooming in front of the house. The shadows of the flowers were swaying in the moonlight. The force of the wind would buffet the door. The sound of its thuds would reach our ears.

There was a typhoon in my heart and thirst had dried out my throat. I got up and picked up the kettle near the fireplace. I drank two gulps of water and peered outside, opening the window slightly. A gust of wind blew into the room. Ripden shivered.

I looked at his face. The old blanket was bunched up around his feet. I visualised Norden running along the sandy bank, dragging his lame foot. His face must have been like that of Ripden's.

"What are you staring at? Haven't you slept?" Ripden asked, kicking me. "Close the window, the wind is getting in!"

I shut the window and turned to my right. The bearded uncle had slumped down as soon as he had finished narrating the story. His deep breaths were bouncing off the bamboo slats of the wall and coming towards me. I raised my head and looked at him. His burning eyes suddenly met mine. I turned my eyes away towards the door. The stench of stale alcohol was in the air. I pulled the blanket to cover my nose.

There was no sleep in my eyes but instead, there was something like a dream; it was limping along a riverbank, dragging one leg. It was, in fact, Ripden's appa. That is, the Norden of this story.

And who was this man who had told us the complete story of Ripden's appa? This thought immediately assailed my mind. I pulled down my blanket, looked at him, reeking of alcohol, and gathering courage, asked, "Uncle, who are you actually? Please tell me!"

Bada yawned for a long time. He coughed twice and said, "I am not your bada. I am your kaka. Call me Nasim-kaka, will you?"

Nasim-kaka? He wasn't Ripden's appa's elder brother but his best friend.

My mouth remained open in astonishment. Only then did my eyes shut. I fell asleep.

*

We tend to dream mostly of things we keep in our minds.

I saw the bank of the river, where I was completely alone. I didn't have slippers on my feet and stones were pricking my soles. Suddenly, someone kicked me from behind. I became helpless. I was pushed into the flowing river.

"Who the fuck shoved me in?"

I opened my eyes.

Surprise, I wasn't in the river but beside the fireplace. Ripden had poured a jug of water on my face. He was also the one who had kicked me.

"Won't you go home, you donkey?" Laughing, he called me names, "Bastard, it's nearly ten. I've been trying to wake you up for long, but you didn't hear a thing."

Tossing aside the blanket, I looked at him. He had come back after digging up chayote tubers. He was smeared with mud.

I turned my head and looked towards where Nasim-kaka was

sleeping, but he had already left.

*

We set off for home at 11 a.m.

We had a bundle of chayote roots and Marie Biscuits in our pockets. When we were about to reach the village of Sinji, the strap of one of my slippers came undone.

Ripden ran into the forest, returned with some skunk vines, and mended the strap with them.

I began to hobble.

"Oi, they will take you to the city to study, I hear." Ripden said, "Will you be able to stay there without me?"

Dense fog had covered the path. Nothing was visible ahead. That fog entered my heart. The state of my mind turned dark.

I thought about Norden who had gone to the town. Will I be able to live without Ripden? I couldn't think of anything. The fog that had entered my heart brought rain to my eyes. My eyes were completely wet.

"This idiot is so sensitive. He keeps weeping," Ripden said, smiling. "I will not study anymore. I will ask for some land for sharecropping and sow ginger. I will raise goats. They say keeping cattle and goats suits someone who has hair all over his body. And my body is hairy!"

My eyes were glistening with tears. Words failed me. He continued, "You study. Class 5 is difficult but Class 6 is easy; Class 7 is difficult but Class 8 is easy. Thereafter, only Class 9 is difficult but Class 10 is easy and you will clear the final easily. And you will become a writer too."

"Who told you this?" I asked hesitatingly, "My grandfather always said the same thing."

"My aku said this."

"How much did your aku study?"

"My aku?" He scratched his head for a bit and said, coughing, "I don't know. The old man doesn't even know how to write his name."

"Really!" I then remembered my grandfather's words and said, "But they say Class 2 of the olden days and Class 8 of now are equal."

He didn't quite get this. He kept walking ahead of me in silence.

We headed down from Jorline at sundown. The darkness had engulfed us when we reached Dalapchand. The moon rose when we reached Biga.

The moon reminded me of a saying by Miss:

"Let us not chase after light alone. Were it not for darkness, the moon, the most beautiful thing in the world, wouldn't have been visible."

Yes, indeed. A little darkness is needed for something bright to be seen.

"Oi, today is Purnima, so the ghosts might be out and about. Take off your sweater and wear it inside out," Ripden said in a frightened voice, wearing his own clothes inside out. "They say a man hanged himself in Pipal Dara. His ghost haunts people there on nights when there is a full-moon or new-moon. We must walk with our clothes inside out. Understood?"

I took off my sweater and wore it inside out. My heartbeat increased. My legs started to shiver. It seemed like there wouldn't be enough light by the moon to walk by.

"What will you do if ghosts haunt you?" Ripden whispered into my ear.

I had not seen a ghost before in my life. What if it really haunted us today? I couldn't think properly. My voice was stuck in my throat.

"We have to swear and use bad words, got it?" Ripden came up with a new idea. "They say our aku also saved himself from a ghost by doing the same thing. Ghosts are supposed to be frightened of stupid people. If a ghost haunts you, you must run towards it while swearing, understood?"

My ears started ringing.

I started to see ghosts in everything. My own breath frightened me, twice. We were about to reach Pipal Dara when I saw a ghost. It was dark, like the stump of the needlewood tree.

Did I have any choice but to swear?

I gathered all the strength in the world and screamed, "Ja . . . an . . . tha bhut! You want to fight? Come . . ."

Ripden must have gotten scared when he heard me scream. That was why he started to utter words I had never heard. I was running and repeating those words when a slap resounded on my cheek. I fell down.

I thought I wouldn't survive. I joined my hands and started crying when another slap fell. That was when I came to.

A familiar voice screamed into my ear, "You'll die, you little fool! Ripden has spoilt you completely. You have started running away from home. You have become someone who walks about at night using bad words! I will break your legs if I see you with Ripden once more. Go to your aunty's house tomorrow, understand? That will set you right!"

I had used bad words in front of my mother. I turned around and looked behind me. Thoo! That ghost was in fact the burnt stump of a needlewood tree.

I melted out of fear and shame. I couldn't say anything other than "yes" to her. Thereafter I don't know how many times her five fingers stamped their mark on my cheeks.

But what I do know was that two days after that incident, I was sent to town to study, carrying a report card that Miss had prepared. In that report, I had received 80 marks in Math, even though I hadn't appeared for the exam.

I walked ahead silently. Baje followed.

When we neared Pipal Dara, my legs went limp and I started shivering. Turning, I looked down at the fields of mustard. Ripden was going towards Kimbugairi with a herd of goats. I was overwhelmed with my love for him. I couldn't control myself. I wept loudly.

That was the last time I saw him. Thereafter, I could neither laugh nor cry with him. I couldn't even see his face.

*

Everything is in a rush in town. Time itself hurries along.

The fifteen years I lived in town were spent in a haste.

Fifteen years after Ripden and I were separated, I stood leisurely on the same land where I took my first step and breath, where I cried and smiled for the first time. That is, I was going back to my village for the fourth time. Now I had to write the story of Ripden, who had written the earliest memories of my life.

The warm rising sun and our childhood are the same. They both enter the world carrying a little bit of light with them.

I recalled those bright days.

The earthquake had cracked parts of Pipal Dara. The fields of mustard had been buried by the mudslide.

I looked towards Ripden's house for the last time. It had been swept away completely. The bamboo grove where Ripden had etched "R+P" had been denuded. Ripden's first love sprang in front of my eyes. We used to call her Pokchi—the plump one.

The villagers reported news of her:

"Pokchi has married a man from Pubung on the far side. She's already mother to five daughters. And is carrying yet again, in the hope of a son."

I was taking pictures of the landslide, controlling the flood of tears in my eyes, when someone patted me on my back and said, "So he's finally come. You've become a big man now, no? What a heart of stone you have. You've forgotten us completely."

A big man?

"A person becomes a dinosaur the day he starts considering

himself important and powerful, and then he disappears," I thought and turned my head slowly.

Ripden's aku was standing in front of me.

"Stones were what I collected to learn how to write." My eyes teared up. "Those alphabets of stone. They were what I studied to understand life. How can I ever become like them?"

A cloud of disappointment swirled in aku's eyes. A landslide of grief swept down his face.

I felt bad. I went up to him and said, "The one who disappears never dies. They will come back every evening in someone's memory. Ripden will never die. Do you understand, aku?"

Aku didn't. Dusting off his clothes he drank a cup of black tea. Then he warned: "Make sure that the news of Ripden's death appears in the paper."

"I came here just for that," I said, taking aku's picture. "He was my best friend. He would do whatever I told him to do. Won't I do this much for him?"

Aku stared at me. I felt suffocated.

I placed the camera in its case and slung the bag on my shoulders. A wiry boy was coming from a little further away, rubbing his eyes. His calves were splattered with mud. His vest was torn, his feet were bare, and his hair was a mess. He walked straight up to me and asked, "Oi, will the Panchayat election be held?"

Lo, it was Juniram, who wanted to be a politician.

"It might. Will you contest if it is held?" I asked, encouraging him. "And where is Hari Prasad?"

"He went to Delhi," he said, taking a long breath. "He is washing dishes in a hotel. You are fortunate. And don't you dare forget us."

Memories are like water in a river that flows down to the sea. It then becomes vapour and mixes with the clouds. The vapour scuds along with the wind and falls as rain into the same river. All one has to do is wait.

"Time takes a person to many places," I said hesitantly, "Some memories are never meant to be forgotten. The memories we share are like that, Juniram."

He bared his teeth in laughter.

I had to note down the details of the landslide, which I did. I had to take photos also. That, too, I did. I finished my work.

What I had left were a few memories that I stored in my eyes.

I reached Pemling after walking for three hours. From there I headed to Kalimpong in a jeep. I had to write out that piece of news.

And then?

I wanted to stick my head out of the window and look up when we reached Relli.

Ripden's aunt's house was somewhere up there. Old memories flooded back. The innocent Ripden smiled before my eyes.

Lo and behold, a new road had been built there. Houses had mushroomed in places where there used to be only forest. It looked different.

"Is Nasim-kaka still alive?"

I suddenly remembered the old man from many years back. I remembered his story again. The same question raised its head in my mind, "Has Ripden's crippled father come back?"

I felt unwell again. I was shocked. My eyes started to flood with tears and my mind with memories.

I didn't know if Nasim-kaka was still crushing stones. I didn't know if he was even alive. I didn't know if Ripden's father would come back. I didn't know if Norden would appear in someone's memory every day.

I only knew that Ripden was not in this world. He had died and he would never return, not even in someone's memories every evening.

The last memory which he had left behind on earth was this *Faatsung*, this song of the soil.

Translator's Acknowledgements

What had first endeared the translator to *Song of the Soil* was the distinct narrative voice and beauty of Chuden Kabimo's prose. The translator would like to thank the editor, Anurag Basnet, for helping him retain some of the beauty of the original.